TRACY DARNTON

READY OR NOT

LiTTLE TiGER

LONDON

That was the day I stopped playing games. You're meant to find everyone in hide-and-seek. Close your eyes and count to twenty. But when I opened them, I couldn't find Kat.

None of us could.

But people don't just disappear, do they?

12 August 2018
Creek House, Cornwall, SW England

I counted to twenty in that droning voice where you stretch out the numbers. Like the way you respond in assembly at junior school – Go-od morn-ing ev-ery-one. I counted like that because we'd been playing this game together at Creek House since we were little kids and started calling ourselves the Creekers. Every August. Every New Year's Eve. When our three families got together in the holidays, we played all sorts of sports on the uneven lawn – cricket, rounders, badminton, tennis. Everyone joined in, sporty or not. And we played board games like Cluedo, Pictionary and Ticket to Ride or mad games of charades and treasure hunts.

But I always loved hide-and-seek the most. It plays to my strengths. I'm good at watching and waiting and keeping quiet. At New Year we played indoors, hiding in cupboards and draughty hallways behind the heavy, dusty curtains. But for our summer visits, we had the garden – terraces, a sloping lawn and dense trees and shrubs which ran alongside the water down to the river beach. The old summerhouse, the log shed, the garages – there were plenty of possibilities and a reassuring familiarity to it all. As we got older, it became only us kids playing games, not the adults. Not hide-and-seek anyway. They'd stay indoors, sitting round the kitchen table with an endless supply of wine, full of gossip and insider jokes, pretending they were still the same people who'd met at university.

That day in August was long and sunny and warm. It was the final day of our holiday all together, our last-night party. We'd downed bottles of cheap cider sitting out on the lawn, looking down at the creek, before dancing like no one was watching. We were waiting for dusk to fall. I'd asked for the game – the older ones wanted to stay drinking and chatting. They did it to indulge me, the baby of the group. Kat pushed me into volunteering to go first.

She squeezed my hand. Her breath was heavy with the smell of the French cigarettes she'd taken to smoking to annoy her dad, who wasn't even there. "No cheating, Mills. I know what you're like," she whispered. She lifted my hands to cover my eyes. "I know exactly what you're like," she repeated, as she ran softly away across the lawn. I watched through my fingers as Matt bounded off and disappeared into the dark of the shrubs before I even started counting. His sister Jem wobbled back in the direction of the terrace, tripping over her own feet. She'd been glugging one of her dad's terrible cocktails. Charlie walked off towards the woods – he never rushed for anyone. Kat began counting loudly in French, shouting as she ran further away. *Un, deux, trois*. She wasn't French, just liked to pretend she was fluent after an exchange trip to Paris. It had only lasted two weeks, but she'd come back with an affected way of shrugging her shoulders and a collection of new exclamations and insults. It annoyed the hell out of Charlie. But they're twins, they thrive on annoying each other.

I began my count at full volume so Kat would stop hers. *One, two, three.* I was already thinking about the next round, about where *I* would go to hide. I preferred hiding to seeking. I was better at it. Maybe I'd take the space hollowed out in the yew – low branches to sit on and leaves so thick that no one could see inside but you could watch other people. I liked following the comings and goings of Creek House. Unobserved.

Fo-ur, fi-ve, si-x.

Things were changing. Mum said it was probably the last time all of us would come in August. It was getting too complicated as us kids got older, with school trips and impending gap years. And Dad hadn't been able to come with us this time because of work. He'd also muttered about not wanting to use up his holiday in the same place, with the same people, every year. But I liked that it was always the same.

Se-ven, eigh-t, ni-ne.

Things had definitely been weird since the twins' parents split up. No more Rob, but a new boyfriend for Liz each time who always tried too hard to fit in. Dom was the current one and way younger than Liz which meant he thought it was OK to engage us in conversation about TikTok and say 'cool' a lot.

Te-n, ele-ven, twel-ve.

A twig snapped and I peeped through my fingers. There was a blur of a tall figure in a dark jacket nearer the house. It couldn't be Matt or Charlie. Maybe Dom had finally decided to abandon the grown-ups for the Creekers. We were more fun.

Thir-teen, four-teen, fif-teen.

I strained to hear what was going on around me. The distant sound of a motorboat, laughter from somewhere towards the old summerhouse, startled crows taking flight, feet running across the grass and the gravel path, whispers. Sound always echoed and bounced around the creek. I tried to build a mental picture of the familiar and the unfamiliar, already planning a route to pick up the others. I'd get Jem first. Her giggling would give her away.

Six-teen, sev-en-teen, eigh-teen.

Time was nearly up. I was dizzy. I hadn't had half as much to drink as Jem, but I was regretting having anything at all. Kat had pushed it on me when I didn't want it, with the usual 'joke' that I was the fun police. But now I was feeling way too fragile to run around after them all as quickly as usual. I would take it slowly. I'd creep up on them in the darkness, silent as the grave.

I stretched out the last seconds like I always did. *Nineteen and a quarter, nineteen and a half, nineteen and three-quarters.*

Twenty!

I opened my eyes and shouted: "Coming, ready or not."

Notebook of Millie Thomas. Private.

When someone goes missing, everything changes. Especially when they disappear into thin air like a magician's trick.

Nothing is the same.

No one is the same.

Dear Kat,

Writing to you is meant to help. Even if the letters aren't proper ones and never get posted and just sit here in my notebook. That's what the counsellor Mrs Edmondson said.

But then she's said a lot of things that were meant to help but didn't.

Seeing Mrs E keeps Mum and Dad off my case. It gets me out of things, like now. Mum was going on again about how I should go out more once my GCSEs are over, meet up with the friends I really don't have.

The girls at school were kind at first, curious. But everyone loses patience in the end, and sympathy gets exhausted. They don't want to hang out with someone miserable. But that's OK because no one else measures up to you on the friend front.

So, this evening, I stopped the usual circular conversation in the best way I know how – I said I needed to write my letter like Mrs Edmondson suggested. Doctor's orders. And Mum and Dad can't argue with that, can they?

Not when they know how important it is, not when they don't want any repeat of the dark days.

Lots of love,

Millie-Moo xxx

P.S. Don't worry. No one will ever replace you, Kat.

As soon as I get back from school, I sense the atmosphere in the house. Kat's mum is here again, red-eyed. Liz is dressed in her new uniform of a big, baggy cardigan and jeans with a stain on the knee. She's huddled with Mum in the kitchen. By the number of empty mugs in the sink, I'm guessing she's been here a while. Today there's no wine bottles but it is only four in the afternoon so there's still plenty of time. And she'll be staying a while. She always does.

I don't want to be a cow, but I wish she wasn't here, that she didn't come all this way to cast a massive dark cloud. Even when Rob left her, she wasn't like this. She was angry and noisy and feisty then. Now she's broken.

And none of us can fix her.

Only Kat.

Mum gives me that look. The one that means I merely say 'Hi' and take a glass of water and a handful of biscuits and retreat to the lounge. I sit on the sofa and pull out my phone.

Kat's details flash up on my timeline in another of the Missing posts. It must be a few weeks since that last happened, but it always makes my stomach lurch when I scroll down and come across her picture. The photo this time is one I remember from her Instagram account. She's wearing skinny jeans and a soft blue jumper with a silver

11

star in the centre. Her hair is straightened, hanging loose on her shoulders, and she's doing the pose; her lips slightly pouting, one leg in front of the other, hands on hips.

Help us trace Katherine (Kat) Berkley, 16. She's white, 5 ft 7ins tall, brown eyes, long red hair with a fringe. She was last seen in south Cornwall on 12th August 2018 but lives in the Bristol area. Any info call 101, ref KB10127.

Kat – if you read this, please let us know you are safe – call your family or 101.
#FindKat

It's been nearly ten months – 302 days to be precise. Why would she call now? And who are all these people who never met her liking the post and passing it round?

Dad's key turns in the lock. It's too late to retreat upstairs before I get the full exam post-mortem.

"Millie, you're back already." He ruffles my hair like I'm five, or a labradoodle. "How did it go?"

"It was OK. I ran out of time a bit on the last couple of questions, but everyone said that afterwards. You were right – unreliable narrators came up."

My parents' interest in my GCSE performance is stifling. The exam timetable is displayed on the kitchen wall like a military campaign with stages to be ticked off. A colossal, colour-coded revision timetable is pinned up next to it, alongside articles cut out of the newspaper, with no sense of irony, about how to cope with exam stress. (*Spoiler alert* – not like this.) A giant 'Good Luck' card sits on the shelf. Highlighter pens, Post-it notes and index cards lie in a box on the table, alongside my 'healthy snacks'. Mum and Dad wrote to my school demanding they ask the exam board for special dispensation for 'all the upset' and the lessons I missed last autumn.

"Have a short break before you get Mum to test you on your French for tomorrow."

"It's fine, Dad. Honestly." I know enough French words to pass the A-level. "Liz is here."

Dad frowns and closes his eyes briefly. "Again. I see," he says wearily. "It's your last week. You need a calm house." He calls to Mum and asks if he can have a quick word. My stomach begins to churn. And it's nothing to do with the exams.

It takes about three minutes for it to escalate. I slide past them and into the kitchen. I close the door between the kitchen and the hall. They're arguing in loud whispers and hisses. If I can hear them, I'm pretty sure Liz will be able to. Except she's lost in one of her moments again. I clear my throat but she doesn't move or look up. She keeps staring down at the glass in front of her. The wine has been opened after all.

I turn on the radio to drown out Mum and Dad. Classic FM fills the kitchen. It's meant to be good to revise to.

I straighten the Polaroid photo on the fridge. All of us last summer. Kat with her statement hair, me mousy brown with a sunburnt nose and Jem, spiky blond hair and tanned. Jem is tall, like her mum, inches above me. Kat's in the centre, as usual, her arms intertwined with ours on each side. Charlie's leaping up to make rabbit ears behind Matt's fuzzy blond mop of hair. They're both in shorts and loud Hawaiian-style party shirts. There's nothing to hint that it's the last group photo we would ever have. We look like we're on the edge of something, the start of our future. We look like we're the best of friends.

Liz barely notices me sit down opposite her. When she raises her eyes, set in sunken, dark circles, she reaches out her hand to mine.

"Millie – dear, kind, Millie-Moo." Her nails are chipped, no polish.

I tense up. "Shall I make you a cup of tea?" I don't know what I should do for her but that's what everybody else does.

Her hand tightens on mine slightly. "I've had enough tea. To. Last. Me. A. Lifetime." She takes two gulps of the wine instead and we sit in awkward silence for a few minutes before she suddenly says: "You'd tell me, Millie, wouldn't you?" Her eyes are focused on me now, her gaze intense. "If you knew anything? Anything at all?"

"Of course," I say, uncomfortable. We've had this conversation before. She's still holding my hand and her nails are digging into the soft flesh of my palm.

"Because I think you *do* know something," she says. Then, in a whisper: "But you can tell me, Millie. Millie-Moo."

I shake my head slowly, try to pull my hand back, but she has it in a firm hold, and her other hand has moved to grip my wrist. "I don't. You're … you're hurting me, Liz. I don't know anything."

"You won't get into any trouble, I promise." Her voice turns into a slow hiss as she squeezes out the words. "We've all made mistakes, trusted people we shouldn't have."

I shake my head again. "I'd have said. I'd have told you if I knew anything at all."

A slow, fat tear runs down her cheek.

As Dad opens the door and sees me, she releases her grip and I pull back my hand and rub my palm.

"Everything OK in here?" he asks, uncertain what he's seen, or not seen. I leap up to fill the kettle, to make the tea Liz doesn't want.

I can't give her anything she wants.

I can't tell her anything she wants to hear.

I promised Kat.

15

Dear Kat,

If you've been paying attention, you'll have seen I'm finding it hard to get you out of my head.

A thought gets triggered when I'd like to show or tell you something.

Sometimes the trigger is a smell. Don't worry – I can see the shock on your face, you who always sprayed half the contents of the Boots perfume hall when you walked through it. I should say scent, not smell. Because last month it was lemons. That lemony shampoo you had – I bought you the matching shower gel and the body spray. They were expensive. You probably don't remember.

So, in Food, Mr Finch was off sick. And this supply teacher told us to research and adapt a recipe involving citrus. She said Vitamin C was sure to come up in the exam, which instantly got everyone's attention. She tipped a bag of lemons on to the workbench and I picked one up and held it to my nose. For ages. Weird, I know.

Because all I could think about was you and the lemony shampoo.

Even in a dumb lesson, there you are. Not leaving me alone.

<u>Ingredients for a one-sided friendship</u>
  Lemons
  Secrets
  Lies

16

Method

Throw all your ingredients haphazardly into a bowl. Mix them up.

Cover with a clean tea towel and leave in a cool place. For a really long time. All your life.

Let it sit. Let it fester.

Every now and then dare to lift the cover and check on your friendship. See if it's the way it's meant to be; if it's growing, doubling in size. Or is it shrinking? Is it rancid and mouldy?

Miss Whatever-Her-Name was quietly reading my 'recipe' over my shoulder. She was disconcerted (my new favourite word). She didn't know what to do with it. That's not what they sign up for, is it, supply teachers? They don't want a situation to deal with.

She edged closer to the utensils and sat casually, or not so casually, by the knife block and fiddled with the buttons on her cardigan. At the end of the lesson, she made me stay behind and suggested I have a word with my form tutor if there was anything troubling me.

Thank God, she didn't know I already see Mrs Edmondson. She'd have been even more disconcerted.

I wrote a recipe, that's all.

Just not the one she wanted. She didn't even give me marks for the clean tea towel reference.

I'm rambling, Kat. But that's what I mean about you,

the absence of you. You pop up in unexpected places. Your thoughts, your laugh, your meanness.

Your lemony shampoo.

Lots of love,

Millie-Moo xx

There was nowhere to hide from the awfulness. It was still sunny outside, still the summer holidays. But inside it was like we were in a TV drama that we couldn't switch off. Liz was in bits, alternating between vomiting and weeping. Rob had arrived alone at 6.30 a.m. after Nick called him. He sat grim-faced and huddled with his old friend, their recent argument forgotten. We'd had enough drama. Mum and Anna had stepped up to provide refreshments and be the shoulders to cry on. Dad was driving down from Berkshire. He'd sounded so shaken up on the phone. I guess Mum, Dad, Nick and Anna were secretly relieved that it was Kat and not their child who'd disappeared into thin air.

The remaining Creekers gathered in the TV room. Charlie flicked through the news channels like he expected Kat to pop up on screen and tell us all she was OK. Matt hugged Jem for what seemed like five minutes and she sobbed on his shoulder. I didn't cry. It wasn't real. Like I was watching us from above.

Dom drifted between the different areas, settling here and there but fitting nowhere. His packed bags sat by the door waiting for his taxi out of there. Once we knew Rob was on his way from the hotel, it was the only option. This was way more crisis than he'd signed up to as Liz's date for the week. To be fair, Dom had been great through the night when Liz was a wreck, organizing us to search through the dark woods and along the creek with torches. He was calm while the rest of us were panicking.

Dom had been the first to say out loud that Kat could have fallen into the water. None of us wanted to think about that. We'd been running along those paths since we were tiny kids. But it was still possible to trip. Especially if you'd had a few drinks. I told myself that the tide was low, Kat was a strong swimmer and used to the river. The water was calm as anything, the weather dry and settled. There was nothing to suggest the creek we loved could have turned killer. But amid an air of unreality that any of this was happening, we had diligently combed the banks and Dom and Charlie had taken out the kayaks as first light broke.

Now the taxi beeped its horn cheerily – as though there was no disaster unfolding inside the house. Dom awkwardly shook Rob's hand and said he was sorry this had happened. He asked Liz to keep him posted, he'd see her when she got back to Bristol, and reached to kiss her on the cheek but she turned away. Normally Matt would have relished watching that love-triangle moment, dissecting it in full gory detail, but even he had lost the appetite for drama.

At some point in the morning a police officer arrived – Constable Shah. She didn't seem that concerned yet. Maybe she would by the evening. I didn't understand how the sliding scale from mild interest to red alert might work.

She stressed that teenagers go walkabout for all sorts of reasons and turn up before long. She asked if it was possible Kat was playing a trick or having a strop or being a drama queen (because that's what teenage girls do, right?).

Liz begged Charlie to tell her whether he thought Kat might harm herself, if there was anything he hadn't told her about. Boyfriend trouble, school worries, an eating disorder, drugs. He shook his head to all her questions. We all reassured her that there was nothing to tell.

With Mum sitting next to me, I described to the police officer what we'd done the previous night. There was irrelevant stuff that I didn't need to mention; private things, like the barbed comments or the amount of drinking. I gave Constable Shah a step-by-step account of hide-and-seek. I said I'd stood by the horse chestnut tree to count, and how I guessed Kat had headed across the lawn from the direction of her footsteps and her voice still calling out numbers. I explained how I'd found Jem first, then Matt and Charlie, how I'd assumed Kat was hiding by the sunbeds or behind the giant planters which edged the terrace. But she wasn't.

I'd checked all the usual hiding places round the front and back of the house while the others sat chatting on the terrace until they got chilly and bored and went back inside. I described how I searched all the hiding places again. How I started shouting Kat's name: "Come out, Kat, I'm getting cold."

I *didn't* tell her how irritated I'd been, how I'd shouted

21

into the darkness: "That's enough, Kat. You've made your point." Or how cross I was, thinking she'd switched off the outside lights to make it harder, or that she wanted to ruin the game somehow, because it was important to me to play it. I'd assumed she was sitting tight somewhere, laughing at me. That as usual she'd found a way to muck things up for everyone *and* be the centre of attention all at the same time.

I *did* say how I'd told the others I couldn't find her and Charlie had shrugged and said she'd come back soon when she got too cold and Matt had suggested looking for a plume of cigarette smoke because she wouldn't be able to last this long without one. And I explained how Jem and I began checking inside the house. The police officer didn't understand why a bunch of teenagers were playing hide-and-seek, why we were playing in the dark and why the house was out of bounds. I didn't like her implying that we were weird. It was a tradition, it was fun. Hide-and-seek was outside only in the summer, unless it was tipping down, inside only at New Year. Those were the rules.

I'd been cross with Kat for not following the rules. You can't have games without rules. Cross with her for turning this into one long, irritating go of me being on and looking for her. So that there would be no time for another round, no time for me to hide. I expected to see her smirking face somewhere in the house. I thought I'd pull back the heavy velvet curtains on the landing and she'd be there, saying: "Boo! What kept you, Mills?"

22

Except she wasn't behind the curtains, or in the cellar, or in the walk-in larder, or behind the baby grand piano. She wasn't under any of the beds or in a wardrobe or a shower cubicle or squeezed inside a linen basket or trunk. I flung back doors and ran between floors, calling her name. Jem and I met up in the hall. She'd shaken her head, and that was all it took for the panic to set in.

"Kat, where the hell are you?" I didn't shout it. I whispered. Because I'd switched from annoyed to scared.

A knot formed in my stomach that has stayed there ever since.

"The police aren't doing anything." Charlie tapped me on the shoulder now, bringing me back to the awfulness. "Matt's going to drive around the lanes and I'm going to walk the woods and creek again. Jem says she'll go to the village and ask around, get Mrs Biscoe to spread the word."

"Good idea," I said, wishing I'd thought of that. Mrs Biscoe had worked at Creek House forever and knew everyone in the village. And her son Noah could help too. I rose from my seat, waiting for my instructions.

"Stay here, and message us if anything happens," said Matt. He picked at a scratch on his hand.

"That looks sore."

He shoved his hand in his pocket. "From a crappy bramble last night playing your stupid game. Keep checking social media while we're gone."

Jem gave me a hurried hug as she left. At fifteen I was the

least useful – Charlie could cover more ground than me, I couldn't drive like Matt, and I was rubbish with strangers while Jem was charming.

Kat had been gone sixteen hours. Hardly any time at all when you said it like that. Less than a day. And every minute, I expected her to come back. Any time a phone rang or a door handle turned, I expected it to be her. Back with some excuse that she'd gone for a walk or fallen asleep, and no apology for all the fuss. But it was heading into late afternoon and the sick feeling wouldn't go away.

I kept replaying every word she'd said, every little thing we'd done the previous day for a clue that she was going to walk out of our lives. When Liz sobbed about someone taking her, about what could be happening to Kat right now, that minute, I couldn't bear to listen. Creek House had felt so safe. There was always a door unlocked to allow for all the comings and goings of our rambling household. Bad things didn't happen here.

I checked my phone again for messages. Kat's Instagram had nothing new posted.

I called Kat's number. It went through to voicemail and her familiar voice said: "*Hi, this is Kat. I'm soooo busy I can't take your call so you know what to do after the beep. Byeee!*" No drama. I left a message, again, to add to all the earlier ones.

I scrolled through my photos and stopped on the last one I took of her – the one I showed the police officer so she could have an up-to-date picture. Kat was sitting in the green armchair which she said looked good with her hair. Yes, she could be that vain. The others were out in the garden, but Kat and I were playing backgammon. One of the dice had rolled off under the sofa and I'd pulled out a humongous, revolting dust ball which had set us both giggling for no sensible reason at all. I was having a good evening. The best in ages. Like things were back to normal. And so was she.

We all knew Kat inside out. We'd have known if she was in a desperate state, known if she was going to do anything stupid.

Wouldn't we?

Dear Kat,

That first day I checked your Instagram account, but you hadn't added anything new. I was already familiar with all your posts. Maybe too familiar.

Dad says social media makes us curate our lives. We share just one side of ourselves. Like your Instagram – @Livresque_KB – means 'Bookish' in French. (I looked it up before you had to tell me.) You scattered a few French phrases around and took arty shots with books now and then. I liked the posts from your French exchange trip best. Dad said they were pretentious when he saw me looking at them, but what does he know, right? I loved the ones in black and white with the Eiffel Tower and the old bookshop Shakespeare and Company

– very stylish.

Your title was very clever, very you – *Livresque: A chat in Paris*

Chat and French for cat in one. Very good. The perfect pretentious pun.

If you don't mind a tiny bit of constructive criticism, now that I have a little distance, more perspective, your posts weren't that original, if I'm honest. A bit too 'Copy Kat'. (I can do pretentious puns too). And way too many exclamation marks!!!!

And the thing is, once you'd decided that that was you (that pretentious, pouting, full make-up, stomach-sucked-in, hair-flicking girl) you tried to be that all the time.

Remember when we used to laze around on the sofas in our unfashionable pyjamas on a Sunday morning waiting for the adults to get up and shake off their hangovers? But last summer... By last summer you wouldn't have been seen dead like that, without your make-up, without your hair perfect.

So, when that police officer asked me if I'd seen any changes in your behaviour recently, maybe I should have mentioned that. But it would have sounded silly, childish, to point out that you didn't like to hang out in PJs with me any more.

Anyway, there were bigger things to think about.

More important things not to tell them.

Love,

Millie-Moo x

26

13 August 2018
Missing: 18 hours

The police searched the house while we gathered in the kitchen. A giant game of hide-and-seek was going on around us. Footsteps thundered on the floor above, doors opened and closed, police radios hissed and spluttered.

Matt couldn't sit still. "How well do they search, exactly? I mean, big spaces or, like, through our stuff too? Drawers and, er, bags?"

"They're looking for my daughter – in human-sized spaces," said Rob. "No one cares about your stash of dope, Matt. They want to make sure we're not hiding her. God only knows why we'd be doing that."

"People do, don't they? Bad parents," said Liz. "People out for attention or to sell their story to the papers."

Rob put a tentative arm around her. "Luckily, we're not bad parents. Let them do their job."

Nobody would give Rob a Dad of the Year prize – least of all Kat. But everyone was too kind, or cowardly, to point that out.

When the police were satisfied Kat wasn't in the house, they started on the garden and outbuildings – the double garage with the chest freezer, the summerhouse, the sheds. They poked through the wheely bins and the compost heaps. They opened the boots of all our cars on the drive and checked the spare wheel compartments.

I didn't want to be there, trapped in the kitchen with so many people and so much emotion. Since Dad had arrived an hour ago, he'd barely left my side, and kept hugging me. It was claustrophobic. Jem tapped her fingers on the tabletop. Normally she'd play the piano to de-stress and I wanted to hear it now, to drown out all the noise from the police unit.

We'd been upgraded from Constable Shah to the gruffer Sergeant Harris telling us what was happening. When he returned to the kitchen after the search was complete and said we could leave the room, Jem was the first into the hallway, taking long, deep breaths.

"Now you've checked we haven't concealed our own daughter," Liz said to the sergeant, "or killed her ourselves and chopped her up to pop in the freezer, maybe you should be out looking for the actual monster who's taken her."

"She's upset," said Rob. "Sorry."

"Don't you dare apologize for me," said Liz.

"Let's all take a breath," said Sergeant Harris.

Mum made tea. Again. No one wanted any tea but they drank it. Clasping a mug gave you something to do with your hands.

Sergeant Harris was doing his best to be reassuring. "Chances are that Kat wanted to escape for a while and she'll be home before we know it."

"Escape what?" I asked, but he didn't answer.

"Most missing people are back within twenty-four hours – seventy-nine per cent of them," he said, in a reassuring voice.

If you got 79% in an exam, you'd be made up. It's a high number. But I concentrated on the other 21%, which also felt like a pretty high number to me. The longer Kat was away, the further she was moving towards the 21%. Kat had been missing seventeen hours already. That was plenty of time to be chopped up and stored in anyone's freezer. And Sergeant Harris hadn't given us the stats for the ones who *never* came back. I obsessed about the figures while Jem chewed her fingernails. Charlie and Matt were quiet – no banter. Charlie was pale and anxious, clicking each of his knuckles in turn.

I'd thought it was easy to find people in today's technological world. I'd thought thermal drones would scour the woods for Kat, and her phone would be easy to trace. I'd watched the movies and TV dramas. Kat's phone was off – we knew that from repeatedly calling it and it not even ringing. Sergeant Harris explained that triangulation of mast signals showed the phone had last been used in this area. We could have told him that. We knew she'd been in this area – right up to eleven last night. We had to wait for Kat's phone to be charged up and switched on again – which seemed like a design fault to me.

"Whenever you were on a video call with her, that low battery message would flash up all the time," said Jem.

"Kat was always running out of charge," I said. "She liked playing music and videos and it drained the battery. That must be what's happened."

The police officer smiled at me, like I was talking rubbish.

But if I wanted to believe that Kat was sitting under a tree watching a film which had drained her battery, I would. It seemed as good an explanation as anything he'd come up with.

All of us hoped that her not answering the phone had a perfectly innocent explanation. The buzz of optimism ebbed and flowed around us.

Mrs Biscoe arrived – like we needed more people to make tea. She said Noah had just got back from his cousin's in Exeter and was joining the search party organized by the local Sea Trout Inn.

Nick had been on his phone calling in favours, lobbying a distant connection in the chief constable's office, insisting more should be happening. Dad whispered to Mum that a lifetime of knowing how to play the system and when to throw money at a problem was kicking into play. Nick was useless at tea and sympathy but the dark arts of networking and getting things done: that was his domain.

But even Nick couldn't solve this problem. The police had said Kat was a Low Risk Misper, or missing person. There was no evidence she was at risk of immediate harm. She was sixteen, not a little kid. And they were doing all they could.

While they made calls and spoke in hushed voices, I watched the clock.

I watched Kat's steady movement out of the 79% towards the percentage who never come back.

Extract from transcript of the interview recorded on Body Cam between Police Sergeant Harris and Amelia (known as Millie) Thomas on 13th August 2018

PS H: Millie, you've been very helpful already with my colleague Constable Shah describing exactly what happened when Katherine went missing, how you spent the evening and where you looked for her. And very helpful in describing what she was wearing. So, thank you for that. What I'd like now is for you to talk to me a little bit about Katherine. I'd like to get a feel for what she was like so that I can do my best to find her. If she needs finding. Is that OK, Millie?

M: She's Kat, not Katherine. She hated Katherine.

PS H: OK, that's good to know. Happy with your daughter helping us out like this, Mrs Thomas? And Constable Shah is going to help me with taking some notes.

Mrs T: I'm sure Millie is only too happy to help but please bear in mind this has been a very traumatic experience.

PS H: Yes, of course. I'll be as brief as I can. I've already spoken to Katherine's brother. And I will be speaking to the other young people too. So, Millie - you and Katherine were good friends?

M: Kat. It's Kat. Best friends. Since we were little.

PS H: And you and your families always get together here in Cornwall in the summer and after Christmas.

Mrs T: Kat's mother and I were at university together, with Anna and Nick. And Kat's dad, Rob. We live all over the place. Anna and Nick are in Islington and we're down in Berkshire. Liz and the twins live in Bristol but Rob's in London now, Clapham, I believe. Anyway, we try to see each other every New Year's Eve and in the school summer holidays. Staying here, at the de Vries family holiday home, has become a tradition. The children have all grown up together through these breaks away.

M: Mainly I see Kat when we're here at Creek House. But we've met up in Bristol or London a couple of times too.

PS H: You and Kat are close?

M: Yes. We pick up where we left off when we get to Creek House. We both like books and playing games.

PS H: And had you noticed any changes in Kat's

behaviour or mood, Millie?

M: No.

PS H: Do you and Kat message each other, when
        you're not down here?

M: Not that much. It's mostly about hanging
        out when we come to Cornwall.

PS H: But you are the kind of friends who tell
        each other secrets, Millie? Best friends
        do that.

M: I suppose. Yes.

PS H: What had Kat confided in you this visit?
        If you shrug, Millie, it's hard for me to
        know what you mean.

M: Nothing. There was nothing special.

PS H: What about a boyfriend? Can you answer
        clearly for me and Constable Shah please,
        rather than shaking your head.

M: No. She didn't say anything about a
        boyfriend.

PS H: Girlfriend, then?

M: No. Kat isn't into girls.

PS H: So, you two friends get together in August
        after not seeing each other since January.
        Seven months. And you don't have a catch-
        up about who you're going out with?

Mrs T: Millie's only just fifteen. She's way too
        young to get started on all that. Kat's

a school year above Millie - and, how do I say, more mature in age and outlook. Millie has her schoolwork and -

PS H: Maybe, Mrs Thomas, you wouldn't mind getting Millie a glass of water? She's looking a little hot. We can pause the interview.

Mrs T: If you're OK without me for a minute, Millie?

PS H: Millie will be fine. And I'd love that coffee you mentioned when I got here. Milk, one sugar. Good and strong, please. *(Mrs Thomas leaves the room.)*

PS H: Now that Mum's gone for a bit, Millie, is there anything you'd like to tell me that you didn't want to say in front of Mum? Shaking your head again. See, I find that hard to believe, Millie. Because you and Kat are best friends. Isn't that what you said? I think best friends tell each other things.

M: Only if there are things to tell.

Dear Kat,

    We were all questioned by the police.

    Do you think they know when you are lying?

    Do they have a lie-detector machine they'll wire me up to one day, or is that only on the true-crime TV shows you like?

    Lots of love,

    Mills xxx

13 August 2018
Missing: 20 hours

Whether it was down to Nick's networks or standard protocols, I don't know, but a police dog team arrived. Kat had been missing twenty hours. It'd be dark again soon. They were going to search the woods and local paths we'd already combed, as had local volunteers organized by the pub. The Cornwall Search and Rescue Team was also involved, so that more ground could be covered. Liz and Rob were clinging to the theory that she'd injured herself on a late-night walk and was waiting to be rescued.

Kat loved dogs so she'd be pretty mad to be missing out on seeing the dog unit. The tracker dogs weren't cute and fluffy like the cockapoo Kat and Charlie used to have. And they were loud. Especially the two German shepherds. They were all straining at their leads, tails wagging, desperate to get started. I tried to stroke the springer spaniel but the handler said I couldn't because the dogs were here to work.

Liz took one of Kat's running shirts from the laundry basket. Even I could smell her from that top, so the dogs reacted as soon as it hit their noses. The barking echoed round the valley as they headed off through the grounds with their handlers. The springer was making a beeline for the lawn outside the summerhouse.

We sat at the table on the terrace, picking at the sandwiches Dad had brought with him from the service station.

"I feel like shit," said Charlie. "Like I've been at an all-night party for days, but without the party."

"Same. There's no way I'd be able to sleep," said Matt. "But don't worry, mate. So many people are looking for her now."

"Can the dogs still follow her trail if she went in the water?" I asked.

"Don't think so. The water dilutes the smell," said Jem. "It was on that film I watched with Kat at New Year."

"The tide was low," I said. "Kat could easily have waded along the edge of the creek to avoid leaving a trace if she wanted to."

"You're making it sound like my sister wanted to get away and was out to make it harder for any tracker dogs. This is Kat we're talking about, not Bear Grylls, survival expert."

"She could have done. Once you eliminate the impossible, whatever remains, however improbable, must have happened," said Matt. "Or something like that – Sherlock Holmes."

The springer was back, her nose skimming the ground, tail wagging, as she followed trails through the garden. Kat had been all over the garden this last week – that's what we did. The dog ended up back at the terrace with us, sitting at Jem's feet and barking up at her.

"Damn. Kat borrowed this top the other night," she said. She pulled the sweatshirt off over her head and offered it to the dog handler.

"We don't want cross-contamination between two people," he said. "It'll confuse the dogs. We'll put this one out of her way and use the original T-shirt again."

"Sorry," said Jem. "I didn't think."

"OK, let's keep working, Pippin," he said, and pulled his dog away. We listened to the barking of the three dogs grow fainter and fainter as they headed further off along the creek. I looked at my watch again. Kat had been missing for twenty-one hours.

"We can't just sit here," said Charlie. "Whatever the police say about leaving them to it. I'll phone round her friends again."

Jem got up too, leaving an untouched sandwich on her plate. "I'll do some more social media and boost the Devon and Cornwall Police posts saying she's missing."

"I'll check local radio and the news channels," said Matt. He slapped Charlie on the back. "She'll be home and

37

annoying the hell out of us all before you know it."

The three of them hurried inside. "And I'll…" I began. But they'd already gone.

I drifted around, picking up snatches of conversation between the adults. Dad hugged me again. Mum was busy hugging Liz. Rob was lurking in the dining room by himself having a hushed phone call with his girlfriend Giselle, still at the hotel nearby. No one should call their girlfriend 'pumpkin'. Nick was fretting about all the work calls he'd missed. Anna was repeating 'I can't believe it. I can't believe this has happened' at regular intervals.

I joined the others in the TV room and gathered up the day's dirty glasses and mugs. The backgammon set was still out on the little table. I sat in the green chair where Kat had been and stacked the counters back in the grooves at the side of the box. One rolled off and slipped down the side of the seat cushion. I wriggled my hand down to retrieve it and felt something metal. My fingers tightened around it and I pulled it up carefully, holding my breath. I had a horrible feeling I knew what it would be.

"Guys!" I said. Then louder: "Guys, look!" I waved my hand at the other Creekers. "I've found Kat's phone."

The battery was dead, of course. We plugged it into the charger and waited, all gathered round in a circle and staring like it was the Holy Grail.

As soon as it had enough juice, it pinged like crazy with all the notifications. But we didn't have her passcode, or the facial identification to open it up. We tried birthday dates, even bizarre random sequences. I tried one I knew she used elsewhere. But none of them worked before it locked for good. "We'll have to hand it in," said Jem.

We trailed off to the kitchen in a procession behind Charlie, bearer of the phone. Constable Shah placed it into a plastic evidence bag, even though the four of us had handled it. "We'll be able to check her recent contacts," she said. "We'll let you know if there's anything helpful."

End of conversation.

We went back to the TV room so Charlie could channel-hop 24-hour news. Wherever Kat was, whatever had happened to her, she didn't have her phone. She wasn't about to call home on it and ask us to come and pick her up. She hadn't heard any of the messages I'd left her. I didn't know if the police could get the passcode and listen to them, look at her photo albums, see who she'd called – and who'd called her. My cheeks flushed hot again thinking about all the frantic messages I'd sent, all the ones me and the others had ever sent, good and bad.

It grew dark as the clock ticked round. Before she left, Mrs Biscoe brought round mugs of soup as though we were all ill. Maybe we were by that stage. I sipped mine between yawns.

It was raining. The kind of heavy shower you can get in the summer after a beautiful day. Any scent Kat had left, any footprints, any clues would be harder and harder to find.

Sergeant Harris knocked on the door to the TV room and stood awkwardly in the doorway. He had an annoying habit of leaning his head to one side when he had anything important to say. The Cornwall Search and Rescue Team had paused their search until the next morning. The dog team were being picked up and the police were leaving for the night.

Jem said it was a good sign because it meant there had been nothing for the dogs or searchers to find. By 'nothing' she meant Kat's cold, dead body. No one said what they were thinking any more. No one told the truth.

"People our age don't go anywhere without their phone," said Charlie at last, breaking the silence.

"Not voluntarily," added Jem.

Vile images of someone dragging Kat off into the dark bushes filled my head. Probably the others' heads too as Charlie turned deathly pale.

"We'd have heard something if … if anyone took her. We were right there, in the garden," said Matt. "We'd have heard a struggle, a scream. You know Kat, she always has an almighty 'Piss off' ready for anyone trying to make her do anything she doesn't want to."

"People who don't want to be traced leave their phones behind too," I said quietly. Charlie didn't reply as he was already heading out of the French doors into the garden. The security lights clicked on, illuminating the terrace and fading off into the lawn. Matt quickly followed him, pulling on his jacket. "Or maybe she forgot it," I called after them. I was trying to convince myself that there were many reasons why Kat might have gone off without her phone and not said a word to any of us.

Charlie picked out a racket from the box of old sports equipment that lived on the terrace. He whacked the ancient swingball down on the lawn again and again. Like it was the face of someone who'd hurt Kat. Finally he stopped, bending forward to catch his breath.

As he came back towards the house, Matt tried to put an arm round him. But Charlie pushed him away and tipped out the sports box, noisily chucking bats and balls around the garden. He pulled out the giant Jenga blocks and lobbed them as hard as he could across the grass. The normally calm Charlie, the quiet, laid-back twin, had a complete meltdown, like a giant teenage toddler chucking his bricks around the playroom. Jem and I stood transfixed, watching from the window. As the raindrops rolled down the pane, Jem placed the palm of her hand on the glass as if reaching out to him, but I balled my hands into tight fists by my side. I dug my fingernails into my palms hoping for that pain to take over. We left it to Matt, the best buddy, to do something, to help him. I was only ever fourth reserve in the friendship stakes. Matt told Charlie to calm down, told him that everything was going to be OK. Even though it wasn't.

One throw after another caught the statue of the angel in

the big flower bed. Kat had said she looked like Angelina Jolie and called her St Angelina. She'd placed a garland of flowers around her head like a halo. Charlie's direct shots chipped away at the plaster. He was treating this like target practice. Maybe it was the closest he could get to being angry with God. One block dislodged the statue's wing, which swung freely. The next knocked it off.

I wanted to break something like Charlie was doing. But he was a boy, he was her brother, he was allowed to let it out. I wanted to howl and scream and bash my fists against the window until the glass broke and cut my skin and made me bleed. I wanted to, but I didn't. I held back.

I hid inside my head.

The clock in the hall struck eleven, every bong resonating through the house.

Through me.

She'd been gone twenty-four hours.

Dear Kat,

We went on a school trip to Cambridge a couple of years ago and saw the clock at Corpus Christi College. It doesn't look like a clock – more a piece of modern art. The strange creature at the top munches away at the minutes. Kind of like an unfriendly grasshopper but it's called a Chronophage. (I expect you know what that means – a Time Eater in Greek.)

Anyway, the clock is only accurate every five minutes. In the gaps, time rushes on or slows or stops entirely. Because the inventor wanted to show that time is relative not a constant. Fluid.

I looked at the clock. I admired its shiny gold workings and the rippling LEDs, and sketched the strange creature. I copied out the Latin phrase which Mr Bull translated for us: 'mundus transit et concupiscentia eius – the world and its desires pass away'.

But I didn't really understand then what the Chronophage was telling me. I didn't understand until _that_ day.

That day when I was watching the second hand tick round. When I needed time to stop so that you could come back, or to rewind so that we never played that stupid game in the first place. When it was the longest day of my life but somehow also the shortest.

That day when you'd gone missing and hadn't come back.

Lots of love,

Mills xx

They don't know I'm listening. I lean quietly against the wall. I am good at this. I missed the beginning of the conversation but now Mum's saying that after what's happened, Dad can't expect everything to be as it was before. It'll take time.

This is a frequent theme. Dad wants to ease Liz and the absent Kat out of the way. So we can play at normal life again.

I wander off to the loo and return. The record hasn't changed.

"I know it's well-intentioned. But you need to take a step back from Liz," says Dad. "I spoke to Anna and she agrees with me. She recommended someone Liz can talk to. A professional – who's not so close to it all as you."

"Maybe," says Mum. "When you think what state Millie was in last autumn, talking to Mrs Edmondson has definitely helped her get back to normal."

I think that's 'normal' in the loosest sense of the word.

As they talk things through, they seem like the calm, sane parents other people have. Like I used to have. They're having a whole conversation with no doors slammed, no raised voices. Polite. Usually they don't seem to like each other very much any more. Somehow all that got lost in Operation Fix Millie.

Now's the time to ask them. I cough and enter the lounge.

"Millie – I was just saying to Mum how proud we are of the way you've coped with your exams and everything," says Dad.

He wasn't saying that at all, but I let it slide.

And 'everything' means Kat. As does 'circumstances', 'all the upset', 'what with one thing and another', 'last summer', 'August' and 'since'. We are excellent at euphemisms in this household.

What he cannot ever bring himself to say is her name: Kat.

Dad pats the seat next to him and I dutifully sit down. "This is a process. We both understand that."

"There is something that'll help me," I begin. They both look up, surprised. "I can't hide away here forever. I've been thinking about it a lot since my exams finished. I talked it through with Mrs Edmondson at school." Everything I discuss with her is completely confidential but my parents are desperate to know what I say to her. Mostly I say very little, but I enjoy the peace and quiet of her room and she's a good source of interesting long words.

"And I've been in touch with Jem, Matt and Charlie." I'd plucked up the courage this week to speak to the Creekers for the first time in months.

"What will help, Mills?" Mum's eagerness is pitiful. They so want to fix this. To be the ultimate helicopter parents and swoop in and make everything better for their only daughter.

Which is why I know they'll say yes to my suggestion.

I breathe in slowly and then I say it: "So, we'd all like to go back for a long weekend? Me and the others."

"Back?" says Dad, cautiously.

I look him straight in the eyes. "Yes. Back to Creek House."

Dear Kat,

My counsellor says sometimes you have to face the bad stuff, tackle loose ends. I tried the whole ostrich head-in-the-sand routine, but it hasn't helped. The feelings haven't gone away by not returning there. By hiding.

Creek House still draws me back.

YOU draw me back.

The others weren't so keen but I talked them round in the end. I kind of lied to each of them and said the others had all agreed. Only a white lie – because they did all say yes in the end.

So, what do you think? A last roll of the dice to fix me?

We're coming back, Kat.

Love,

Mills xxx

16 August 2018
Missing: 80 hours

I was up early. Our room had felt so big and quiet these last few days without Kat in it. Her bed was neatly made which never happened in normal life. Anna had offered to put me in with Jem but I wanted to stay where I was. It was our room, ready for when Kat came back.

But her absence hit me as soon as I woke up every morning and looked across at the empty side of the room. Today was the last day of waking up here. Dad had run out of days off and Mum said it seemed like the right time to go back to our own house. Liz and Charlie were going back to Bristol. The police thought it was best for them to be at Kat's home in case she'd gone back to where she had school friends and contacts.

But it was hard to shake the feeling we were abandoning her.

I slipped out into the garden and walked down to the beach. Mum and Dad had forbidden me from going anywhere alone in case there was a mad axe murderer on the loose. But I couldn't stay in 24/7. It was too claustrophobic, even for me who'd always loved being there.

There was no one else down by the water. I saw a flash of blue as a kingfisher flew low along the creek, and an egret waded on the opposite side of the water. Nature didn't know that it wasn't allowed to carry on being beautiful.

The early paddleboarders and rowers were out, sculling in pairs or singles while the tide was high enough. I liked the sound of the blades in the water and the way people's voices carried from far round the bend. Noah Biscoe rowed past. I nodded at him but he didn't break his stroke. Other people were getting on with their usual daily lives, search parties over, while we were all stuck in this limbo of not knowing where Kat was and if she was OK.

As I walked back to the house, a car drew up on the gravel drive. I watched from the side as the police officers got out. Sergeant Harris's expression was grim. Something was wrong.

I ran back inside, slipped off my damp trainers and rushed back up the stairs. I didn't want to hear any bad news. If no one told me, it wouldn't exist. Liz began to wail downstairs. I stopped still on the landing. The police *had* brought bad news.

"What's happened?" Charlie shot out of his room as Dad was coming upstairs to find us.

"Let's gather in the kitchen, please," Dad said.

"Dad?"

He put a gentle hand on my arm. "Liz and Rob will speak to you all together."

Dad knocked on Jem's door and I went to get Matt while Charlie ran downstairs.

When we were all assembled, Rob cleared his throat and began. "It's nothing definite," he said, as Liz wiped her eyes

48

with a tissue. "But they've found a female body, washed up further round the headland beyond Powan. With the tides, there's a possibility it might be Kat."

"A faint possibility," said Dad.

"They've made an appointment for us to look at the body later this morning," said Liz.

This wasn't real. I clenched and unclenched my fists. Kat was too loud and full of life for that to be her. You didn't drown at sixteen and get fished out of the sea. No. No. No.

*

What do you do for hours while you're waiting for someone to check out a corpse? I mean, it's not something you ever expect to do. If you're an adult, you drink tea in the kitchen and have hushed conversations. Turns out if you're a Creeker you go down to the river beach. We waited, flicking stones into the water. Jem dabbed a crumpled tissue to her eyes and hugged her knees as she gently rocked from side to side. Matt tried to distract Charlie with an endless one-sided conversation about football. He held his phone up high to find a signal in case Liz and Rob called. I stared at my watch as it ticked up to their appointment slot at noon.

We were all there together but not together at all.

"If it's her," said Charlie suddenly, and choked up too much to finish the sentence straight away. He threw more pebbles into the water. "If it's her and she fell in the water and was too drunk to get out…"

"The tide was low," said Matt. "And she wouldn't have gone swimming after drinking. She's not stupid. We don't even know she came down to the beach. It won't be her, mate."

"If she stumbled into the water, knocked her head maybe, she could have been washed out into the estuary," I said, and instantly regretted it.

"Not helpful, Millie." Matt glared at me. "Shut up."

We fell back into silence.

I got to my feet and scuffed circles in the pebbly sand with the toe of my trainer. "Kat wouldn't have gone away without telling me," I said.

"And that's meant to reassure me, is it?" said Charlie.

"Though I suppose if she did bang her head…" I added, trying to work through the scenarios in my own way.

"Enough already," said Jem.

"If it is Kat's body, Millie," said Charlie, "and she died playing your stupid, childish game, hiding in the dark because you'd pestered us into it, this is on you."

He glared at me like he hated my guts.

I ran away, back up the path from the beach into the trees, blinking back tears. Matt called after me, but I kept on running. They probably all blamed me. Charlie was right – if we hadn't played hide-and-seek, this would never have happened. And if she'd had an accident, we'd never have heard her because we were blundering around looking for her nowhere near the water. This *was* on me.

I stumbled back towards the house, not caring that I was getting scratched by the branches. When I reached the garden, I didn't want to go in and face the adults. They'd be thinking exactly the same thing as Charlie. Instead, I melted into my hiding space under the yew tree and sat in the shade, waiting.

Mum came out on to the terrace clutching her phone. The bearer of good or bad news. She shouted across the garden for us. I waited until she went back inside before I came out from under the branches. I didn't want her to know that I was alone, that the Creekers blamed me.

When I entered the kitchen, Mum looked up at once. "It wasn't Kat, love. Rob phoned."

"How can they tell? If she's been in the water for days…"

Mum shifted uncomfortably. "We don't need to get into all that. Take it from me, it wasn't Kat. It was someone else. Older and bigger."

I saw the image in my head of a body on a slab, like on TV, with Liz and Rob looking through a glass window as the white sheet covering it was pulled back. A grisly game of Guess Who? being played out.

"Who was it?" I asked. "Who was she?"

"I don't know," said Mum. "Some other young woman. The important thing is it's not Kat. Let's not dwell on it."

I was happy, even though *somebody* had died. It wasn't Kat and that was the important thing. Even Mum had said that.

"Another family mourning her tonight," said Dad. "Someone who got out of her depth in the water maybe. Makes you realize what's important. That family's all that matters."

He pulled me and Mum in for a hug, but Mum stepped back. "I need to find Charlie and put the poor boy out of his misery."

"I'll go," I said. "They're down on the beach."

"Such a good girl, Millie," said Dad. "Be quick. Bring them back up for something to eat. Charlie felt too sick earlier."

I made my way back down the path, slipping in my eagerness to get there. I wanted to tell them the good news and be redeemed. Kat hadn't drowned and it wasn't my fault.

My phone vibrated in my pocket as I reached the woods. Maybe Mum with something else she wanted me to tell the others. Or Dad checking I hadn't been abducted from the garden as I'd been out of his sight for five minutes. But it was an unknown number. I wouldn't normally answer except … these were exceptional circumstances. No one else was around.

"Hello?"

There was silence at the end of the phone.

I whispered, my heart pumping: "Kat? Is that you?"

9 August 2019
Missing: 362 days

I get a taxi from the rank outside the station in Cornwall. It's good to be back. Despite the reason. It's been nearly a year. We'll be leaving the day of the anniversary, the twelfth, so Charlie can spend it with his parents, lunch with his mum and dinner with his dad. In some ways so much has happened in these last twelve months and in others nothing at all.

As I load my bag in the boot of the taxi and say: "Creek House, Powan, please," the previously silent driver is suddenly interested.

"Ooh, isn't that the house where the girl went missing last summer?" she says.

I don't speak. My face tells her nothing. But she can't take the hint that Kat's off limits.

"Terrible thing. Did you know her, then?" she asks, showing no sign of starting the car.

"No, I didn't. Not at all." I put on my headphones to end the conversation as I slide into the back seat. People are curious. But not as much as they used to be. Kat's becoming old news. Every year 180,000 people go missing – that's a lot of zeroes in a rolling-news world.

Though most of those 180,000 are found safe within twenty-four hours.

Unlike Kat.

The taxi driver plays a local radio station. It's a weird sensation, being back here, travelling through the familiar roads to a soundtrack of 1980s soft rock. The hedges on either side of the narrow lanes are full of flowers and life, rising up like a tunnel. We pull over for a tractor with a trailer full of sheep. I used to like that we couldn't hurry down here. No more school run and after-school activities and tutors and dashing around from one thing to another. We had to take things more slowly. Or maybe time passed differently in the cocoon of Creek House.

We never spent the whole holiday hanging round the house and grounds – though I'd have been happy with that. We'd have trips to the northern beaches for the others to surf and we had some favourite places to go. If it rained we went to the Eden Project or Tate St Ives. The oldies had restaurants they liked to go to as a break from cooking, where we'd eat fresh fish caught that day and sit at wooden tables in the sunshine. There was no better place to be. All of us agreed.

As the taxi passes through the village, squeezing past a badly parked Range Rover, I notice the Sea Trout Inn has the usual holidaymakers with loud voices and bright trousers enjoying the beer garden. The oldies liked it for the occasional lunch in the summer and a cosy quiz night in the winter. The windows of the two art galleries are packed with coastal paintings in shades of blue and green. Wooden birds on sticks and driftwood sculptures stand to attention.

There's a queue at the coffee kiosk next to the gift shop where I used to buy cheap souvenirs.

We didn't count ourselves as tourists, though. We were better than that. The fact that Anna and Nick owned the house gave us all a sense of entitlement and a reason to tut at the actual tourists, or grockles and emmets as Nick called them, in their caravans, clogging up the lanes or queueing for an ice cream in the village.

We were always our own exclusive club, whether we were spending the day at Creek House or out. Loud, sprawling, treating the restaurant or café like they were lucky to have us. Kat said last summer that we'd become the worst kind of people – careless people like Daisy and Tom in *The Great Gatsby*. I probably nodded and breathed in her superior cultural references and marvelled at how clever she was to express it so. I *liked* being part of the careless people.

That was then.

We drive out of the village and back along the lanes, past the sign to the farm shop. Butterflies flicker in my stomach. We're nearly there.

The taxi stops at the drive. The gate's shut. Nick had to get a lock fitted after reporters kept knocking on the door. They called themselves reporters but some of them had just come to stare: gawkers and ghouls. "Here's fine," I say to the taxi driver. I don't want her to have the satisfaction of taking a good look at the house. I don't want us to be gossiped about. I pay her and add a tip like I've seen Dad do.

I wait until she's driven off before trying to undo the combination lock on the gate. I thought I knew the number but it's not working.

My hands shake with the nervous energy of being back and wanting to get in the house and settle myself before the others arrive. A cyclist is heading up the lane and as he comes into view, I realize it's Noah Biscoe. He's more muscly than I remember but still has a long, pinched face. I don't really want to speak to anyone but it's too late, he's seen me.

The bike flicks gravel as he brakes. "All right? Mum said you were coming back for a few days. Molly, isn't it?"

"Millie," I say, embarrassed that he's never bothered to learn my name properly. That's me, so unmemorable. Though I suppose the only occasion he spent time with me was when Kat dragged me along to the pub last summer as the unwelcome extra, and she flirted outrageously with him all night.

"Sorry. Millie, of course. We've been over to open the house up, put food in the fridge. It was pretty sorted already for all the viewings. Scented candles, flower arrangements, the lot."

"Viewings? What viewings?"

"For the estate agents. Loads of people were interested in buying the place despite, well, you know. Mum said the latest lot made an offer way over the asking price and Nick and Anna have accepted it. Mum's met them already. Going to completely refurb it even though they're buying most of the contents too. Be loads of extra hours for me helping round the grounds and Mum as a more permanent housekeeper." His voice trails away as he looks at my face.

So *that's* why my parents agreed so readily and went on about closure. It's one last time. Anna and Nick are selling Creek House. Why didn't anyone say anything when I was arranging this trip?

"They can't sell it!" I say. "What about … what about…?" The words won't come out.

"What about her, you mean," says Noah, looking down. "Kat."

Unlike my parents, he says her actual name.

I'm trying so hard not to cry. I wanted Creek House to be here forever. Like a set we walk on and off.

"I suppose it's lost the holiday vibe. The de Vries family have barely come down in the last year," he says. "Look, I'll come in with you and make sure you're OK with the alarm and I'll make up for putting my massive size twelve feet in it." He undoes the padlock and holds the gate for me. "The number's changed on this and the house alarm. After all those different people traipsed around with the estate agents, we thought it was a good idea."

'*We*' thought. It's not *his* house to think about.

We walk up the drive together, him pushing his bike and

me struggling with the weight of my bag. Mum was right that I overpacked for a long weekend. But what do you pack to revisit the scene of your best friend's disappearance? What's the perfect set of outfits?

"We're not here on holiday," I say. "We're here to remember Kat." It matters to me that he knows we're not here to party.

"OK," he says. "It's really none of my business."

Noah must hate us all. Stuck-up rich kids he and his mum have cleaned up after for years. And the tabloids plastered his face on their pages as a suspect when he got questioned by the police because they thought he'd had some stupid, brief thing with Kat. He wasn't even in the area when she went missing, but the papers didn't print that part.

We *are* all his business, more than he ever wanted us to be. He'll always be bound up with Creek House.

"Who's buying it?" I ask.

He stutters awkwardly. "Another family from London. A banker, I think. Pots of cash to spend on the place. New kitchen, bathrooms. A pool."

"A pool? You can swim in the river. When the tide's in."

"Can't lie around with an inflatable unicorn and a cocktail, though, can you? And the creek can be murky. Bankers probably like their swimming water warm and blue."

I pause as we round the bend in the drive and see Creek House bathed in sunlight, as lovely as ever. I've missed the place so much, despite everything. I grew up here. Roses wrap around the front of the house and the door is framed by giant stone pots of agapanthus flowers. If a child drew a beautiful dolls' house, this would be it. I don't understand how Anna and Nick can bear to sell it.

Noah clears his throat. "Have you, er, been back since … last summer?"

I shake my head.

I used to be pulling off my seat belt as we turned into the drive, itching to get inside and see the other Creekers. Now, I'll be the first to arrive. Charlie's driving down and picking up Jem from the station. Matt will be here later because of some hockey thing somewhere he can't get out of. I didn't want to wait, preferring to get the earliest train down I could. By tonight all the Creekers will be together again.

All except one.

Dear Kat,

There are lots of firsts you have to get through when someone leaves your life.

The first birthday – yours and mine – they were pretty bad.

The first Christmas without you – not much festive fun. Mum and Dad massively overcompensated and bought me loads of stuff I didn't need and they couldn't afford.

They didn't mention you at all.

You were the elephant in the room. Or the Kat.

Mum phoned your mum which was even more of a downer to the day.

I didn't mind about Christmas Day so much because we've always had that with family but afterwards was odd. Because we didn't drive down to Cornwall. We didn't go to Creek House. That was a horrible first too. The first time ever that we hadn't been there at New Year. I went to a party with someone from school. My mum arranged it with her mum. Humiliating. I left by 10:30.

No one went to Creek House. Your mum was busy with her breakdown and your dad was busy with his new life and Charlie was busy getting into trouble instead.

Jem and her parents stayed at a friend's place in the Lakes. The Italian lakes, not Windermere. Jem has no end of friends with glam holiday homes. And Matt – I don't know. He doesn't keep me informed about his life. Jem said he was revising for his A-level mocks with school friends but I find that hard to believe.

We all did our own thing.

So, maybe you were the one who bound us all together, Kat. You were the centre of our Creekers' universe, and we all revolved around you. And now we're all drifting off into different orbits.

I'll be honest, New Year was better at Creek House. Everything was better there. Until ... well, you know.

Love,

Mills xx

LOCAL LONER QUESTIONED
ABOUT MISSING GIRL

Police investigating the disappearance of holidaymaker Katherine Berkley have taken into custody a local man, said to be known to the police.

Sixteen-year-old Katherine Berkley from Bristol was holidaying with friends in the popular and picturesque south coast area of Cornwall. She disappeared last Sunday during a late-night party at the creekside holiday home of well-known City financier Nick de Vries and his wife, magazine editor Anna Channing. Extensive searches of the local area have been conducted.

Landlord of the Sea Trout Inn, Powan, Ali Ninan, said "Many of my regulars stepped up to help look for the young woman – we're proud of our community spirit here. Nothing like this has ever happened before."

Local sources say that the man assisting the police with their inquiries works for the de Vries family at Creek House. Neighbours described him as "A quiet lad", "A misfit" and "A bit of a loner".

Liz and Rob Berkley, Katherine's parents, are separated and thought to be returning to their homes in Bristol and London. They asked that people continue to look out for Katherine, whilst respecting their privacy at a difficult time.

"We are pursuing a number of lines of inquiry," said a Devon and Cornwall Police spokesperson. "We are appealing to the public to report any sightings of Katherine."

Katherine is described as a white female, 5 ft 7 in in height, of slim build, with long red hair. She was wearing a blue-and-white striped dress, green jacket and white trainers.

Police have asked that anyone with information or sightings of Katherine should contact them on 101.

9 August 2019
Missing: 362 days

Noah helps me with the key safe and alarm then leaves. We swap numbers in case there are any problems with the house. I'm not very subtle in hinting that I want to be alone. I practically bar him from coming inside by standing in the doorway waving goodbye. Anyway, he has a shift at the Sea Trout.

I've never actually been here by myself before, all alone in Creek House. That was part of the appeal of our holidays – it was always bustling and crowded and noisy, there was always someone to talk to or hang out with or watch. Not like home at all. But I want to take full advantage of the time alone today. This has been my happiest place but also my saddest. The best of times, the worst of times.

I go round every room, my hand trailing over the furniture to mark it with my presence, like a cat. The hall is grand and wide – the kind that looks good with a Christmas tree and neat rows of wellies on the tiled floor. The grandfather clock has a dent where Matt ran into it on his skateboard when he was twelve. The kitchen's huge with a massive wooden table by the windows leading to the terrace at the back. It has the middle-class essentials of a walk-in larder, an AGA and a huge fridge. There's still room for two sofas and shelves of artfully arranged white crockery and cookery books. Everything looks as though it's always been there, slightly faded or comfortably shabby, even if Anna bought it recently. Kat said you have to try really hard with interiors to look like you don't try at all.

The formal drawing room has an impressive fireplace and a high ceiling. I called it the 'lounge' once and Anna corrected me. The fire is piled up ready with logs, even though it's August. The paintings are all scenes of Cornwall, picked up by Anna from galleries in Marazion and St Ives. Not the ones in the village. The room is full of a carefully curated collection of mismatched armchairs and sofas. The baby grand piano takes up one corner. Jem complains it's never properly tuned but her playing sounds pretty good to me. You could find a room like this in any one of Anna's glossy magazines lined up on the oversized coffee table.

The dining room is barely used – except for marathon games of Monopoly and the New Year's Eve formal dinner. It's always the coldest, darkest room except on special evenings with a fire roaring and all the candles lit. Mrs Biscoe and Noah must have set it up to look good for potential buyers as all the places are set with the best china plates and sparkling cutlery and glasses. I take a silver napkin ring from the table and pass it from one hand to the other before slipping it into my pocket.

Further down the hall, there's the 'library'. It's a tiny, book-lined room with one armchair and a reading lamp, converted from a large cupboard. The TV room is where the Creekers spend a lot of time. The massive screen and games consoles are here, along with cupboards of board games, table football and a pool table. It's far enough away from the drawing room and the kitchen that the oldies can't hear what we're doing, and leave us alone.

Nick grandly calls the boot room full of walking stuff 'the map room'. He has neatly filed baskets of Ordnance Survey maps, even though he's normally too busy to come out with the rest of us. One wall is taken up by a map of the local area which we've all doodled on over the years. The adults have done useful things like highlight favourite footpaths and walks to pubs. We Creekers had our own set of symbols like an ice-cream cone marking where to get good ice cream, Kat's fluffy sheep in fields or Matt's doodled seals and shark fins off the beach.

A conservatory packed with wicker furniture and a 1920s cocktail cabinet that looks like something from an Agatha Christie drama completes the ground floor. But the oldies like it in there, so we don't use it much. Lastly, there's the door to the cellar with a creepy staircase straight out of a horror film. It's always cold and damp and cobwebby – which makes it a rubbish place for hide-and-seek. The door creaks on its hinges and the wooden stairs groan like a sound effects department. It's for cardboard boxes and broken stuff that never comes out again.

Easy to see why I called Creek House the Cluedo house when I was little. The pool table definitely qualifies the TV room as the billiard room. We did our own fancy-dress Murder Mystery party one New Year's Eve, moving from room to room to make accusations. I loved it.

I carry my bag upstairs, stopping on the first floor. This has the bigger, grander bedrooms where all the parents sleep, and Jem has a room at the front with an old four-poster. I check out all the nooks and crannies. I select a perfume from Anna's dressing table to spray around in suffocating clouds. I try on the silk dressing gown hanging behind the bedroom door and waft along the landing.

It's good to act like Creek House is mine before Jem and Matt arrive. It's their family holiday home after all. Not that they ever appreciated it like I do. And now they're abandoning it. I won't be able to walk around it, lie on the beds, poke into cupboards and open drawers I shouldn't open. If it were my family's, I'd persuade Mum and Dad to let us move in permanently and I'd finish school down here. I'd never want to sell it. Especially now.

I climb the narrower stairs to the top floor where the kids' rooms are. Our rooms. I go straight to the old armchair on the landing and pat the lumpy cushion to reassure myself before I push open the door to the massive twin room where Matt and Charlie always sleep. It's stuffy and I throw open the window, looking down the drive, half waiting for the others to arrive.

I hesitate before entering our room. Kat and I always shared what Anna calls the Blue Room. The wallpaper, the curtains, the carpet are all blue. She sticks with the theme and makes sure the bedding matches. It's like going to bed in the sky and the sea all rolled up into one.

Kat used to make fun of me for saying that. "It's more like sleeping in the old-lady section of the charity shop," she said. "But Anna thinks it's charmingly vintage, so we're stuck with it."

We're at the very top of the house and it gets impossibly hot in the summer and freezing cold in the winter. The cluster flies like it and as usual I spend my first few minutes opening the windows and flicking fly carcasses off the ledges. This room has the best views even if it has the lowest ceilings, looking out across the garden as it slopes down to the water and the wooded hillside beyond. You get glimpses of boats or rowing sculls on the river through the gaps in the trees.

We have our own bathroom with a creaky shower over the bath and a curtain that flaps and clings to you as you stand under the water. Kat moaned but I like it more than our immaculate bathroom in our boxy new-build home back in Berkshire. I think it's better to have character than to be bland, better to be different than the same as everyone else.

I know other people stay here – Anna's brother and his family for starters. Sometimes we'd find a piece of Lego or a sock left by Matt and Jem's little cousins. But they were only visitors in *our* room. This was our world. Mine and Kat's.

The two beds have been made up. I guess Mrs Biscoe's giving me a choice – or maybe she didn't think about whose bed she was making and what it meant. The room looks ready for Kat to walk in here, throw her bag on the bed and go straight to the window to shout down to the boys on the terrace. I unpack my clothes, and carefully put my notebook under Kat's pillow, put the toiletry bag in the bathroom I won't have to share with her any more. The whole house is full of ghosts of the past, but in here it's overwhelming. I sit on her bed and gently smooth down the cotton pillowcases. If I close my eyes, I swear I can hear Kat laughing.

It's funny how someone's absence can fill a room.

There are patches of paint in varying shades of white and grey on the wall, breaking up the blue. Fabric swatches are scattered on the mantlepiece. The carpet's been pulled up in one corner to expose the floorboards and there's a mood board from Cornish Luxury Interiors propped up against the fireplace. The people who want to buy the house must be planning a major makeover in here. They don't even own the house yet and the Biscoes are letting them come in and redesign it. I pick at the board and the stuck-on images of twin brass beds and new, smart furniture. Looks like nothing in this room is staying. The window seat where Kat loved to sit is being reupholstered and the carpet's to be replaced by stripped floorboards and expensive rugs. It won't be the Blue Room any more. Every last bit of mine and Kat's time together growing up in this room is going to be 'disappeared', erased from history.

A car horn beeps a couple of times and I run into the boys' room at the front. It's Charlie driving his seventeenth birthday present from his dad. The guilt gift. Jem and Matt follow closely behind in Anna's VW. They came together after all. I whistle and wave down before heading back to our room.

It's still our room for this last weekend so I gather up the fabric and the mood board and pull open the biggest drawer at the bottom of the chest of drawers to ram it all in out of sight. But the board catches on something that's slipped down the back of the chest, blocking the drawer from sliding back. I reach my arm in and grope around until it settles on something solid and I pull out a thick, padded envelope bound with an elastic band.

I thought I was the one who was good at hiding things.

Jem shouts my name downstairs. I quickly tuck the padded envelope under my mattress.

Creek House still has secrets to share with me.

Dear Kat,

You were in my head a lot today. Even more than usual.

Sometimes it doesn't feel like you're missing at all. Because your presence is so heavy. The weight of you pushes me down.

I'm just about managing to stay afloat most days but on others you're forcing me under, no matter how hard I try to keep treading water.

You have to let me breathe.

Love,

Mills x

P.S. I found something today. I slipped it under my mattress.

I knew there would be things to find. I knew.

5 August 2018

I'd been so looking forward to seeing Kat and everyone, and for the holiday to start. Mum had taken forever to drive down, hitting the holiday traffic and stopping at too many places on the way without Dad to share the driving. I hated being the last to arrive, knowing they'd all been holidaying without us already.

There was no sign at all of Kat. Jem seemed genuinely pleased to see me, steering us into the kitchen with her straight away, though she rolled her eyes when my mum called her Jemima. She was wearing loungewear – the type of clothing that makes me look like a shapeless dollop but makes Jem look like she's fresh from a yoga class in Chelsea. Her hair had been cut really short and she nervously ran her hand across the back of it. "So glad you're here, Mills. Things have been…"

"What do you think of my little sister's army buzzcut?" interrupted Matt, squeezing me round the waist and planting a kiss on the top of my head. His dad jokes that Matt has a magic mirror in the attic somewhere giving him eternal good looks. All through his teens, he only ever had one single spot appear; he christened it Boris and poked at it fondly as though it was rare and unusual. Matt was full of chat about Glastonbury and how he was completely ready for a spell at Creek House, living off his parents before his A-level year and uni applications.

He was always buzzed to have Charlie to hang out with. Theirs was a friendship played out by throwing a Frisbee to each other, kicking a football about or endless table-football championships. Or they'd huddle together sharing something funny on their phones. They showed affection by remorseless piss-taking and complicated high-five manoeuvres.

Charlie made a fuss of me, as though me arriving was the highlight of the day – which of course it wasn't. "Millie! Mills! Millie-Moo! What's new?" He picked me up and swirled me round like he did when I was tiny. What was the cut-off age for him to do this – sixteen, eighteen, forty?

Kat still hadn't appeared, but Anna was the perfect hostess as always; asking how our journey was, making sure our rooms were ready, laying out drinks and cake in the kitchen. Though it was Mrs Biscoe running round in the background doing most of that, being as inconspicuous as possible. Nick waved from the garden, his phone clamped to his ear. He was always busy, doing deals I didn't understand but knew created the money to fund everything else he and Anna did. Mostly, he was loud and like a shouty City-type character walking in and out of scenes in a play. Usually walking out.

Liz was beautifully dressed, the life and soul as usual, kissing me warmly. My pushy mother asked Liz and Anna if they'd ordered champagne for GCSE results day in a couple of weeks. And whether Jem and the twins could give me some tips. I smiled at Jem who smiled back. She knew what my parents were like.

We'd already had a cold drink before Kat made an entrance. She was barefoot, in a strapless maxi dress and with her hair piled up on her head in a messy but stylish way. Her hair was as long now as Jem's was short. Matt pulled Charlie away to play table tennis. Kat floated across the room, greeting Mum with affectionate hugs and kisses on both cheeks before she reached me.

"Mills. Finally, the band is back together again. New top?"

It had seemed a good idea in the changing room with my mum but now, around Kat and Jem, it felt like a pointless exercise. Like I'd tried too hard and failed.

"It's sweet on you," Kat said and pulled me in for a hug. "Mills. So good to see you." And I think she really meant it.

These were always the best times – when we all pretended to be genuinely pleased to see everyone else. There were high-pitched squeals and bursts of laughter and affectionate slaps on backs. There was the promise and anticipation of a great week ahead before petty squabbles and bad weather and the reality of three families adapting to live together after months apart kicked in.

"I'm exhausted," Liz said, collapsing on to the sofa. "Bring me wine, urgently."

Mum made the mistake of asking: "Why so tired? Bad journey?"

"No, we all drove down last night," she said. She lowered her voice, but not much. "Relentless," she said, pausing in the middle of the word to give Mum a knowing look. "Relentless. I'm struggling to keep up. Getting too old."

Jem stuck her fingers in her ears and said, "La, la, la. I'm not listening." She headed out into the garden to join the boys.

Kat ignored her mother and went to get something from the fridge. It was like Kat and Charlie's parents were in a competition to the death to find the most inappropriate partner. And we now had to share our holidays with Liz's latest effort. The accountant she brought last December farted his way through dinner without apologizing. Matt fanned his nose with the place mat and we gradually got the giggles going round the table. When he went outside to smoke a cigar we rated him out of ten. Even Liz had joined in. Two and a half and I think we were generous. He didn't have much of a sense of humour and left on the 30th. This current one *had* to be better.

"I've sent Dom for a run. Burn up some energy, if you know what I mean," said Liz. "You can meet him later."

"I'm sure we can't wait," said Mum. "Twenty-nine, you said? I've got jeans in my wardrobe older than that."

"He's a creative, you see," said Liz. "All that time at art school has given him an appreciation of the beauty of the female form."

Kat slammed the fridge door.

"Anyway, don't *I* deserve some fun?" Liz spat out the word 'fun' like it was the exact opposite. "Am *I* not allowed my own midlife crisis?"

"I should really go and unpack," I said. "Kat, do you want to give me a hand?"

We exchanged a look. She knew I was helping her get out of there.

I was her knight in shining armour.

9 August 2019
Missing: 362 days

The late sun streams through the windows in the big kitchen/diner. The sunlight makes patterns through the glass vase of flowers in the middle of the table. The pattern is more interesting to me than the flowers.

Dinner, or 'supper' as the Creekers always call it, is a selection of deli items supplied by Mrs Biscoe. I set out a pile of knives and forks and five plates in a stack on the table. I'm not used to 'hosting'. I can't even remember when I last had anyone round to my house. But I like playing hostess here.

Supper is subdued. It doesn't feel right to be loud or boisterous. We haven't been together since last August and we don't click like we used to. The fifth plate sits empty on the table. Everyone has glanced at it, but nobody says anything or clears it away.

Charlie can't sit still. His leg jigs constantly and eventually he gets up and walks around the room, picking things up and placing them down again. He's putting all of us on edge. Charlie is like Kat in the way their noses turn up slightly at the end and they both have long limbs and the ability to curl their tongues in a basket shape. But as for personality, he's the exact opposite. Or he used to be. Charlie's open and honest. He's a graceful loser and happiest outdoors or playing sport. He doesn't see why you'd read a book unless you absolutely have to and doesn't hold a grudge or even get annoyed about much. Which annoyed Kat because grudges were her speciality. Charlie's smiley, he likes messing about and having fun. If I could have had a brother, I'd have picked Charlie. The *old* Charlie. Because *this* Charlie is not the same at all. I wouldn't pick this one.

"Maybe this wasn't such a good idea," he says, looking at his trainers rather than any of us. "Millie said we should mark the anniversary but it's so weird to be back. Creek House looks as it always did, everything's strangely normal, but…"

"But everything has changed," I say.

Jem is up straight away, sticking her arm round him. "Hey, we're all here for you."

Matt snorts. "God, spare us that, Jem. No group hugs. Apologies for my little sister. What this situation needs is a beer." He opens the fridge and pulls out a couple of bottles. Matt and the kitchen are not best buddies. He opens random cupboards and drawers noisily searching for the bottle opener until I can't bear the racket and fish it out of the utensils jar for him. "Cheers. Seek and ye shall find," he says, as he flicks the bottle tops on to the floor. He gulps a mouthful of his beer and hands the other to Charlie. "Here you go, mate."

"Last time I checked there were four of us here. What about me and Millie, you sexist git," says Jem. She shoves him hard in the shoulder on her way to the fridge.

I shake my head at the offered bottle.

"Come on, Millie. Loosen up. Mummy and Daddy aren't watching," says Matt.

Jem pulls some bags of crisps from the cupboard and throws them on to the table.

"We're not here for a party," I say. "We're here for Kat."

"It's not a *party* party. Though I'm guessing you don't have much experience of those. It's more a kind of memorial, isn't it?" says Matt. "Isn't that what you wanted?"

"You have a memorial service when someone's dead," I say.

"Exactly," mouths Matt.

We all look at Charlie. He's picking flaking paint off the window frame, looking out across the garden. The horse chestnut tree where I counted for hide-and-seek stares back at us. I wish they'd chopped it down.

"Isn't it more about 'closure'?" says Jem. "Millie was right to suggest we come back. Everything last summer was so mad afterwards. We never really got to sit together like this – without the parents hanging around – and talk it through. And especially now Mum and Dad are selling the place. We never got to say goodbye to Kat. Not properly. Not here."

"Goodbye? What are you talking about?" I say. "You only use goodbye if someone's not coming back. Like the difference between *Adieu* and *Au revoir*, remember. Kat taught me that."

"In her French phase," says Jem, raising her eyebrows. "*Ooh là là.*"

I glare at her.

"What?" she says, pretending she wasn't being mean.

"Now we're all here, whatever our reasons for coming, doesn't anyone think we owe it to Kat to find out what happened to her," I say.

"What do you think my family have been doing all year?" says Charlie. "Jesus Christ, Millie. Do you even know how much the police have done? Or private investigators, missing people support groups, mental health charities." He counted down through his fingers. "Her classmates. Every contact and useful connection my mum and dad could call on."

"What could we do that hasn't already been done?" asks Matt. He pokes at his teeth to dislodge a bit of crisp.

I chew at my lip. "Being back at Creek House, I feel like we shouldn't give up hope."

Charlie sighs. "You think the police didn't go through it all with a fine-tooth comb? You know all this already. Sniffer dogs, search and rescue. They searched the house, the grounds, the creek…"

When Charlie lists everything like that, he makes it seem impossible that we could find any answers. But I can't let it go.

"They could have missed something," I say. "A scrap of clothing, a cigarette end…"

"It's been a year, Millie," says Jem. "Any idea of how much rain there is down here – plus badgers, foxes digging about. And we all looked for her too – and people from the village. The police did further searches of the creek in September, with divers. So many people tramped through the woods. There's nothing left to find."

"We know this place better than the police," I say. "We've been exploring every corner of it since we were little."

I look at Matt to back me up, but he shrugs. "I agree with Jem and Charlie. "There was nothing to find then. There'll be nothing to find now."

"So, we give up on Kat, do we? Abandon her?" I say.

"No one's saying that," says Jem.

"People don't just disappear," I say. "There's always something."

"We've all been through a lot," she says.

"Why are we all here, then? Why did you bother coming?" I ask.

"Not so *you* could have a Poirot in the library moment," says Charlie. "I came because I need to move on from feeling this crappy all the time. I thought it might help. And it's the last chance before the place is sold."

Seems like I'm the only one who didn't know about the house sale.

"Moving on. Yeah," says Matt. "Absolutely. Literally in my parents' case. They can't bear to come here any more. Me and Jem are here to say goodbye to Creek House too, to our childhood holidays." He opens another bag of crisps and chews noisily. "Anyone else think we'll never find out about Kat? *That's* what we might have to learn to live with. That's real deep stuff right there."

"Some of us seem to be finding it easier than others," I say, under my breath.

"Not knowing is awful, though," says Jem. "Sometimes…" She hesitates. "Sometimes I wish we'd found her, even if…" She looks at Charlie.

"We'd found her body, you mean?" he says. And we all hold our breath and watch him, waiting for him to kick off. His foot digs at the skirting board where there's an old dent. "Sometimes I think that too. Not at first, but as this has gone on and on without any answers. On Monday it'll have been a whole year. Twelve months. Three hundred and sixty-five days. Mum is clinging on to this idea that I should have some sixth sense or something as a twin about whether she's still alive." He puts both hands on his stomach. "That I'd *feel* it here if she was dead. So therefore she must be alive. That's what Mum's hoping. But I don't feel anything. I'm numb. Unless I'm hitting something. So, yeah, sometimes even I think that bad news would be better than no news."

He slumps back on the sofa after his long speech. I don't know what to say to him.

"The way I see it," says Matt. "And bear with me on this one. Don't bite my head off." He points his bottle at me.

"The way I see it, after all these months is, a) Tragically, Kat's dead or b) Kat's alive *but* she left of her own accord and doesn't want us to find her. She'll come back *if* she wants to. And it's looking like she doesn't want to. Not yet anyway. Who thinks it's A?"

"You're taking a *vote*? On whether Kat's dead?" I splutter.

"I'm gauging opinion. A show of hands. Option A?" He sticks his own hand up.

Jem mouths 'sorry' at me and slowly raises her hand.

"Option B?" says Matt.

"Jesus, Matt," says Charlie, but he still puts his hand up. "Alive. That's what I prefer to think."

"You missed out C: what if Kat's very much alive but *can't* get back to us. That's not in your multiple-choice quiz, is it?" I say, folding my arms rather than play his game. "What if she needs our help?"

"If she's been taken by someone, it's a year on, and I'm sorry to say she's ninety-nine point nine per cent likely to be, well, *gone*. Dead," says Jem, putting her arm round me now.

Taken isn't the right word. It isn't strong enough. Snatched, seized, grabbed, abducted. No one knows. "Stop saying that she's dead. She's not dead until there's a body. There's no body."

"This is like Schrödinger's cat," says Matt. "Kat's neither wholly dead nor wholly alive until we open the box. Option A and option B are equally valid until we find the opposite is true. Until we open the box."

"What box?" asks Jem. "I don't get it."

"You shouldn't talk about Kat like that! Don't you want to find her alive and well?" I say.

Matt sighs heavily. "We all want to find out what happened to her. Of course we do. But we have to be realistic. And we have to face the fact that we might never know."

I feel sick. Physically sick. Charlie pulls me to sit with him and wraps his arms around me in a tight hug. "It's all right, Mills. We all miss her."

"I tell you one thing for sure," says Jem. "Kat would have loved this. A few days here, no oldies…"

"And her the complete centre of attention," adds Charlie, with the hint of a smile.

"And crisps. She bloody loved crisps," says Matt.

"Especially cheese and onion," I say, sniffing.

And we sit quietly for a while, each remembering her and days we had at Creek House.

I can't share the hazy times, the memories that are out of my grasp. I choose to share the time I twisted my ankle running down the path to the beach and she helped me hop home, leaning on her shoulder, and sat me in a corner of the kitchen with a bag of frozen peas on my leg. And when we had a mammoth game session working our way through every board game in the cupboard from 8 a.m. to midnight.

"Do you remember when she went mad at Charlie and me for daring to use a tiny bit of her expensive sun cream?" says Matt. "She was fierce."

"And when she made me and Millie do karaoke for *hours*," says Jem.

"You loved it really," says Matt, flicking a crisp at his sister.

"The rest of us had to watch it," says Charlie.

"And listen!" says Matt. "My ears will never forget that."

"Remember when she did the world's most complicated treasure hunt with about fifty clues. It took forever," says Jem. "And it was only her and Millie left in the end, traipsing round the house and the rest of us were slumped on the sofa consoling ourselves with a tin of Quality Street."

"That hideous jumper she bought Dad that last Christmas before he left," says Charlie, shaking his head.

"Who knew gifting jumpers could be passive aggressive, right?" says Matt.

Charlie laughs. "She made him wear it to church, to parties. The power of guilt. He wore it here at the New Year's Eve party."

"The vibrating snowman?" says Matt, smiling. "Yeah, I remember. Hideous."

"God, she spent days researching that jumper. That's my sister: thorough."

Even I sip at a beer, though I don't like the taste – and Charlie's doing his best to get through them all himself.

It's actually nice. I am having a nice time with the others. Charlie's relaxed his coiled-spring pose and is joking around again. Talking about Kat like this seems to stop her forcing her way into my head without asking. Maybe marking the anniversary with this weekend was an excellent idea of mine. For the first time since that night last summer, we've properly remembered her. The real Kat. Not the one in the missing posters who looks so perfect. That Kat belongs to other people and not to us.

That Kat doesn't belong to me.

Dear Kat,

Your twin is a mess.

Did you think about that?

Did you know that he'd be lost without you, that he's missing a part of himself?

Because he's a boy and you're a girl (I like to state the obvious) I didn't really notice it as much. I mean, I knew you were twins. 'The twins'. That was the shorthand for you when we were younger. But then you and Charlie are so different, I kind of forgot. Liz and Rob never dressed you in identical outfits – though you'd have totally rocked it. Maybe as those creepy twins in the matching blue dresses from The Shining. Hilarious.

But as we got older, you were hanging out with Jem, with me traipsing along behind, and Matt would be with Charlie and we became the Girls and the Boys in the adult shorthand. 'Where are the Girls?' 'Are the Boys in the garden?'

Who exactly was brother or sister, or twins, didn't seem

to matter. That's what I told myself. The only one who was truly alone.

But I see now that you always had a club of two with Charlie, even if you chose at times not to be a member. The twins. Invincible twins. Team twin.

Twins have a connection. A sixth sense. He tries to deny it. But I notice these things.

You'd be very touched to see it now — even if it is burning him up from the inside out.

Even though you guys used to argue like cat and dog, like brother and sister.

Especially that day.

I notice these things.

Mills xxx

5 August 2018

Kat and I were in our bedroom at the top of the house. My favourite place to be. She'd been no help unpacking, of course. Just watching and commenting on my clothes as they came out of my bag. I'd tried asking her about her mum's new boyfriend, but he was a no-go area.

"Why bother? He's done ten weeks. He won't be around for much longer. They never are. Mum's too intense. She thinks some guy who's using dating apps to get a quick shag can replace Dad." She picked up one of my tops and held it against herself in the mirror, turning from one side to the other before throwing it back on my bed. "This 'family' holiday will be the end of it, you watch. I give Dom three days here max. Mum is too suffocating for someone like him."

She flopped on to her bed and spread her arms wide. "I'm sick to death of dealing with my parents' foul-ups. I might go travelling, Mills. Back to France, rent an attic in Paris. Read poetry, write books." She propped herself up on one elbow and flicked her hair. "Be an artist's model."

I stopped unpacking. "You're sixteen. You've got sixth form, uni…"

"You sound like my dad, or, worse, your dad."

"You can't go now. We always said we'd go interrailing together after my A-levels. The two of us. Head for that Greek island from *Mamma Mia*."

She sighs. "That's three years off, Mills."

"You'll feel better after the GCSE results. It's nerves."

"No, I won't."

"It won't be as bad as you think. If it's too difficult they move the grade boundaries."

"You don't get it. I've definitely failed them." She sat up with her head in her hands. "I didn't do them, OK. In the first one I wrote '*This is not an exam*' until my hand hurt."

I couldn't believe what I was hearing. This was *Kat* – the high-achiever. "But French – you're brilliant at French. You smashed the oral back in March. You told me."

"I filled the written paper with '*Je ne regrette rien*'. Line after line of it. '*I regret nothing*.'" She half laughed, half sneered. "I thought I was being very clever, at the time. Existential. I wrote nothing at all in the rest of them."

Dad would hit the roof if I did that. He might even self-combust. "But you've worked so hard. You had extra tutors. What about the sixth-form place at that amazing boarding school you wanted to go to. The posh one? Don't you have to get certain grades?" I hadn't paid enough attention to exactly what grades at the time as I knew for sure Kat would get them.

She stood up and opened the window, pushing the panes out wide and breathing in deeply. "That school's also amazingly expensive. Dad's already said there won't be enough money for school fees any more after he's wrecked our family. So why give him the satisfaction of controlling where I go? This is my choice now." She slumped on to the window seat and leaned her head against the frame. "It was so unreal, Millie. That first exam, I was in there looking at the paper and all these thoughts filled my head about why was I doing them. I was a hamster on a wheel running as fast as I could to please Mum and Dad, to keep them happy and proud of me. But all that turned out to mean nothing. Dad left us – after all that crap about the importance of family for my whole entire life, he ups and trades Mum in for a younger version. All that rubbish he'd fed me about exams and studying and doing your best. I mean, it's so hypocritical."

I kept quiet during her long speech. I already knew she was furious about her mum and dad splitting up. It was her ongoing stuck record. Kat couldn't forgive anyone, ever.

"How dare he put me under that pressure, Mills? When *he* couldn't even stay married for the rest of us. She's only six years older than me. She was in sixth form when I was in Year Seven. Shagging the babysitter – what a pathetic cliché he is."

Her voice wobbled. All I could think of was how she hadn't told me about her exams before. She hadn't shared it while she was actually sitting them. Results were only a couple of weeks away now.

Kat pulled a crumpled packet of cigarettes and a lighter from her pocket. I didn't know she'd started smoking. Her dad was always very anti-smoking, making a show of coughing and waving his hands in front of his face if ever we were within twenty metres of a smoker on the beach. Her hands shook as she lit up.

"Have you told Jem?" I asked.

"No, I haven't. She's been rather irritating lately."

I knew Kat would realize I'm a better friend than Jem. "What do you mean?"

"It doesn't matter. *You* are such a good listener, Mills. God knows I've had a shitty time of it with Dad. What he's done to Mum, to me, to Charlie…" She sniffs. "It's tragic. And now he's dumped me and Charlie and gone off to live with Little Miss Perfect Tits. Maybe he needs a shock to bring him back to his senses."

I didn't have the right words to make any of this better. I hated this world of adults behaving badly. They were meant to be, well, the adults in the room.

She blew smoke out of the window. She was sitting too close to the ledge, leaning out too far.

I moved towards her; my arms outstretched. "Come back in, Kat. You could slip and fall."

"Who would care, Millie? My parents wouldn't. They don't care about me. They're both too busy with their love lives."

"I would. I'd care. I do care. I…"

She reached over and placed two fingers on my lips. "Stop," she whispered. "You care too much."

My eyes welled up.

"Silly billy Millie," she said wistfully, pulling away her hand and turning back to the more important task of smoking her cigarette.

Dear Kat,

That police officer last year expected that we messaged each other all the time. That's what friends do.

But you were always too busy to reply to all my messages. Or call me. I always keep my promises, Kat. But I don't think you do.

I had a long list of excuses for you. Desperate, I know.

Maybe you were too busy being popular; your parents had restricted your screen time; your internet was down; my internet was down; lack of data...

I had loads more.

Excuses. I understand that now.

I guess I've learned this year that I always liked you way more than you ever liked me.

Love,

Silly billy Millie x

5 August 2018

Matt and Charlie were in garish Hawaiian shirts ready for Anna's summer supper on the terrace. It was a tradition that on the first night back together we all dressed up and ate outside, whatever the weather. Matt's shirt had pink flamingos and Charlie's was all purple sunsets and palm trees. "Wow, dude. Respect," said Matt. "You have outdone yourself. I definitely need my shades to look at your one."

Charlie flopped on to the grass. "Some of us have natural bad taste, and some of us don't. Suck it up, Mattie."

"We should get a photo," said Jem. "The annual group shot, while we remember."

"We need the photographic evidence because in ten years' time you will not believe that you went out in public dressed like that," said Kat.

"I'll take it," I said, getting to my feet.

"Then you won't be in it, Millie-Moo," said Kat. "Can we do a few with your instant one, Jem?"

Jem shouted up to the adults on the terrace. "Can you bring my Polaroid camera off the table and take a pic of us guys?"

"We need a good backdrop," said Kat.

"Oh Jesus, it's only a picture," said Charlie. "Not a magazine shoot."

Kat pulled him up off the grass and positioned him with the house in the background. "Why does Matt get out of it?" asked Charlie. Matt was showing no sign of moving.

"Nobody gets out of it," said Jem, pointing to where her brother should stand.

Dom and Liz walked across to us with the camera, holding hands.

"Look at you all, my darlings," said Liz. "So gorgeous. Good job we have a real photographer here to do you justice."

"It's an instant one," said Kat. "Super-easy."

Dom smirked. "Any idiot can take one of these, right?"

"Your word, not mine," she said back, with a broad grin.

Kat was in the centre; her arms round me and Jem. Matt and Charlie messed about. "Say cheese and onion," said Liz.

The Creekers were back together.

10 August 2019
Missing: 363 days

The house is quiet. The others aren't up yet. The clock in the hall, the water in the pipes, the birds. All the familiar sounds of Creek House first thing in the morning that I've known since I was tiny. All except one – there's no roommate breathing and snuffling.

I reach under the mattress and pull out the padded envelope, laying it in front of me on the bed. It isn't mine to open. I turn it over in my hand. It could be more wallpaper samples but something tells me it isn't. Looking at someone else's private stuff is OK if it's less than ten seconds. There's a rule about that. Or that's what I tell myself. I take a quick look inside – and immediately close it up again. At least I know it can't belong to the little Lego cousins. Not unless they're way more disturbed than your average junior school kid.

I shudder and put it back, out of sight. But once you've seen something, you can't unsee it.

*

I pad around the kitchen in my bare feet, shaking off my uneasy feelings. This room should be busy and bustling with all of us – *all* of us – making plans for the day, passing cereal boxes and milk cartons. I liked it like that, the way

I could slot into the crowd here. I pick out ingredients from the larder and the fridge. I haven't baked cookies since last summer. Kat always cooed over them, stealing them from the cooling rack before they'd had a chance to firm up, shedding crumbs across the floor. She was never good at waiting for anything.

I weigh out the ingredients, remembering the recipe by heart. Mixing the dough, forming it into balls between my hands, calms my thoughts. I can sense Kat at my shoulder, hear her swinging legs hit the wood as she sits on the breakfast stool, watching, impatient for the cookies to be ready. I set each ball on the baking sheet, pressing the top down gently. I should bake more often. Even if Kat isn't here to eat them.

While the cookies are in the oven, I switch on the radio and clear up. I am doing well today. Honestly. I can cope with being here in Cornwall and seeing Kat in all these places, sensing her. Her presence is not as scary as it is at home, in the night. I'm lost in a flurry of optimism that I'll be sleeping better, making friends, fulfilling my dreams; all without the spectre of Kat literally haunting me.

But then a track comes on the radio. The one she played that night, the final night, when she turned up the volume on Charlie's phone and swayed her arms above her head and made me dance clumsily with her. And my hands start to shake and I know there's no way I'm ever going to get her out of my head.

She won't leave me alone.

I don't know how long I stand there but the cookies are overdone, black and wasted. I burn my hand getting them out in a hurry but it's pointless rushing as they're already ruined. There's nothing I can do.

Kat's laughing at me, sitting on the stool again, her feet thumping against the wood. *Thump, thump, thump.* A banging in my head.

I need to get out of here.

I reach the horse chestnut tree before I realize where I am and that I don't have my shoes on. I sink down by the trunk and place both hands on the bark of the tree where we always counted. I imagine her feet sinking into the damp ground there, her body leaning into the tree, hands over her eyes, fingers wide because she never liked complete darkness. I count, like I did that night. Counting through the numbers. Until she disappeared.

I breathe in and out, counting my breaths now, like Mrs Edmondson showed me. This is the way I get rid of Kat. Counting is the way to make her disappear. Again.

Minutes pass. The sun is already hot on my face. Matt calls out through the window: "Mills? Coffee?"

When I go back inside, he's poking at the mess in the bin. "They still smell good, Millie. I'm tempted." He picks one out and flicks off a chunk of rubbish. "See, fine. Charcoal's good for you."

"Eww. You are such a savage," says Jem, checking her

phone as she eats cereal. She yawns and stretches out. "What are we going to do today?"

Matt shrugs. "It was Millie's idea to come. What do you do on a semi-memorial minibreak?"

I hadn't really got further than the four of us getting here and being at Creek House. "We could write up a schedule on the board," I say. "All choose something to do."

"It's a weekend away not a boot camp," says Matt. "We don't want a schedule – that's the whole point of being away."

"How about a last-night party – for old times' sake," says Jem. "Not with a party vibe, obviously. But something to remember Kat before we all leave here for good."

"We could have the last night on the beach with a bonfire. Like we used to in the winter," I say. None of us will want to rerun last summer's dancing and games. "Maybe we should wait for Charlie and see what he wants to do?"

"I think Charlie will be sleeping off his hangover," says Jem. "You should talk to him, Matt. If he's drinking like that every night…"

"It's the first night back here, cut him some slack. And like he's going to listen to me."

"God knows why, big brother, but you're the only one of us Charlie *is* likely to listen to." Jem pours more coffee and cradles the cup in her hands, blowing on the hot liquid. "Otherwise, this weekend is going to turn into *Five Get Pissed in Cornwall* rather rapidly."

"Four. There are only four of us now," I say.

"Kat would like the book reference," she says. "And what was it she said when we found that dead squirrel once?"

"Life isn't all *Anne of Green Gables*," I say quietly.

"Precisely," she says, smugly smiling over at me as if she's proved superior knowledge of Kat, when she hasn't at all.

Matt tips up his cereal bowl to finish the dregs. "I'm not the touchy-feely one in this room, but maybe we should do something today that Kat liked to do. If this is all about remembering her. And getting over her. For Charlie."

"Lounge around the garden? Sit on the beach and throw stones?" says Jem. "Ooh, I know! Paint our nails and straighten our hair?" She ruffles Matt's hair and he gives her the middle finger.

"Games?" he says. "Kat loved to play games."

"As long as it's not hide-and-seek ever again," says Jem and shudders.

She heads off to get showered and Matt loiters while I clear up. "I was thinking, Millie, that given the state of Charlie, we should be careful what we say to him. There's no point upsetting him over the past now."

I fill the dishwasher and let him wait for my answer.

"Charlie's in a bad place as it is," he continues. "He needs us to buoy him up. He needs his friends."

"His *friends*?" I say, with as much of an edge as I dare. "I'm sure as his *friends* we'd never do anything to let him down."

He blushes. "Look, Millie, we need to think about Charlie now."

"Did I hear my name?" Charlie bounces in, looking fresher than any of us.

Matt slaps him on the back. "Looking good, my man."

I leave while they're mutually bonding over the cereal choices.

While Matt's pretending to be his best friend.

NO LEADS IN DISAPPEARANCE OF
YOUNG TOURIST ONE YEAR ON

As the one-year anniversary of the disappearance of teenager Katherine Berkley approaches, police say they have no further leads. Katherine is still being treated as a missing person.

The small community of Powan was rocked when Katherine disappeared from a party at the holiday home of her friends, the de Vries family. Although a local man of interest to the investigation was questioned by police, no charges were ever brought and no trace of Katherine was found despite extensive searches of the local area.

It is understood that Creek House has recently been put up for sale.

Katherine's mother, Elizabeth Berkley, still lives in Bristol and has no plans to return to Cornwall. "It's too painful," she said when contacted by the *Cornish Herald*. "But while there's breath in my body, I am praying for my daughter's safe return. I am waiting for her to walk back into our lives one day. We all love her very much and just want her home."

A Devon and Cornwall Police spokesman said that anyone who thinks they may have any information on Katherine should contact police on 101.

Dear Kat,

Did I tell you about when Mum walked me to the pond in the park round the corner from our house and gave me a stone to throw into the centre? It was a thinly veiled allegory about you disappearing and the effect on all of us. Or maybe it was a metaphor. I was always hazy on the difference.

Stay with me on this, Kat. Mum read it somewhere – the stone is you disappearing, and the ripples that radiate out are all of us – the Creekers and our families. But Mum couldn't remember the whole thing properly and it got a bit lost in translation. We threw a few more stones, we watched the ripples, but I'm not sure they were epic enough.

This outing was for me to understand why I'm the way I am, your mum's a complete wreck and your brother got cautioned last month for criminal damage when he had an argument with a bike shed.

Damage.

We're all damaged.

Mum wanted me to feel better. But it's too late for that.

Way too late.

Lots of love,

Millie xxx

10 August 2019
Missing: 363 days

I call out that I'm going for a walk, but they won't really miss me. I'll get to the village and back before the boys have even decided what we're doing. As I cut across the terrace, I stop and stare, a shiver running up and down my spine. The book Kat was reading that week last summer, is on one of the sunbeds. Like she's been out here relaxing in the morning sunshine. I pick it up and hug it to my chest, before turning the pages that her hands turned. The others wouldn't even spot it, wouldn't realize its significance. They don't know what she was reading, the kind of books she liked.

Only a true friend, like me, would know.

I pop the book back inside the house. Matt and Charlie are still bantering for Britain.

I move quickly through the garden, my feet slipping on the rough path. I stare at the ground like there will be something to find that the police missed, that everyone missed.

The sun breaks through the clouds and I tie my sweatshirt round my waist. When Dad was made redundant a while ago and had to give back the company car, we walked a lot. He said it was a chance to get fitter, but I knew it was a way to save money.

The narrow path to our river beach weaves down through the trees. No doubt we'll hang out there later. I take the other path towards the village, heading across our boundary, the gate marked '*Private Property. Keep Out*' banging shut behind me. It joins the public footpath which carries on along the creek. As I reach a stile, I rest on the top step in the growing heat and soak up the view. I catch a glimpse of the tiny creek cove called Tide Beach below with the sunshine glistening on the water. I haven't been down to that cove for ages. Why am I marching all the way to the village when I could paddle in the water and skim stones?

There's a full dog poo bag swinging on the fence post on the narrow route down and it's nowhere near as nice as our beach. But I take off my trainers and tuck my socks neatly into them. I gingerly step into the water, dodging the sharper pebbles. I wade in the shallows along the beach towards the stone boathouse. It's less run-down than I remember. The roof tiles are new and the paintwork's a bright, shiny red. As I'm looking at it, as though the force of my mind has unlocked it, the door opens.

And Noah Biscoe walks out.

He starts, then frowns.

"Hi. Sorry if I made you jump," I say. "You probably weren't expecting to see me, or anyone."

"No, I wasn't," he says.

"I didn't realize this was yours," I say. "And the beach. Am I trespassing?"

He locks the door and puts the key carefully into the zip pocket of his jacket. "My grandad owns it. But he's in a home now, so…"

"You've done it up."

"It was going to fall down otherwise."

"That's clever of you – I've never even painted a wall. No DIY in our house."

That came out like we always have someone in, staff to do such menial tasks, when I'm trying to say we live in a new home and we haven't had to do anything. And that I'm impressed. Instead, I sound like a patronizing rich kid – which makes me gush even more. "I'd love to see what you've done."

"It's only an old boathouse. Like a big shed with a boat in it."

He has a yellow file of papers tucked under his arm which my eyes are drawn to. He sees me looking at it and colours slightly, tucking it further back under his arm as though that's going to hide it.

"What have you got there?"

"What's this, twenty questions?" And he moves slightly to stand more in front of the door.

Whatever's in the boathouse isn't just about his DIY skills. There's something he doesn't want me to see.

Which makes me want to see it.

But I can play the game. I dry off my feet and pick my way back to the path with him, acting all friendly. Charades is one of the games we used to play at New Year. And I'm good at pretending.

6 August 2018

We arranged the sunbeds and parasol on the lawn below the terrace. The sky was a pure blue and it was forecast to be an uninterrupted hot day. The boys had taken the paddleboards out first thing while the tide was right. Kat had decreed that the girls were having a relaxing day of reading and lazing around and playing cards. She said she'd rather stick pins in her eyes than spend the whole day with Matt and his football chat. Kat was loud and confident again. Our talk about exams seemed to have taken place in a parallel universe. Jem was subdued, setting up her sunbed next to me rather than Kat.

I tugged at the straps of my swimsuit, regretting that I'd brought it. It was designed for actual swimming and smelled of chlorine. When I'd pulled it out of my suitcase, I realized it was wearing thin at the back, so I kept my shorts on. It wasn't a lounge-around-in-sunglasses kind of swimsuit. Kat stretched out in the full sun in her white bikini – a collection of four triangles in a shimmery, metallic fishnet somehow held together with four gold rings and thin white cord. She looked gorgeous, of course. It was hard not to stare.

"A gift," she said when she saw me looking. "You seem ready to do twenty lengths, Mills."

"We should do a swimsuit makeover next time we go into Truro," said Jem. I knew she meant mine and not hers.

Her leopard-skin-print bikini looked as expensive as five of my swimsuits and had a matching beach dress which she pulled off and folded neatly to one side.

"You'd suit a black bikini – with padded cups, Mills," said Kat. "They can give anyone a cleavage."

I shrank back into the shade.

Kat fiddled with a headband, also new, pulling her hair back from her face. The tiny, printed seagulls settled into the folds of her hair.

Jem picked up my book, bent back the spine and fanned herself with it. "It's so hot today. Not even a breeze."

"What I'd give for a pool to cool off in right now. In a fancy hotel somewhere," said Kat. "Even though I'm not sure this bikini top would survive any actual breaststroke." She picked up the bottle of sun cream and sprayed her stomach and legs.

"I like it here," I said. "There's the creek if you want a swim. It wouldn't be a holiday without all of us together."

"Aw, bless!" said Kat.

I closed my eyes, laid my arm across my forehead and inhaled the coconut smell of the sun cream. I *was* having a good holiday, even if my swimsuit wasn't glam enough.

"Do you think we'll bring our kids here?" I said out loud and regretted it. I should have kept that thought in my head.

"Shoot me if we're still coming here every August and New Year when we're ancient," said Kat. "No offence, Jem.

But I don't think I'll be doing New Years with the oldies again, thanks very much. Last year was enough. Charades with your mum and dad, Millie, is not my idea of fun these days."

"Agreed. Sometimes things have run their course and come to an end," said Jem. "The world doesn't revolve around Powan and Creek House."

But it did for me.

"I thought… I thought we'd be friends and coming here forever," I stuttered. "Like our mums."

"Oh, Millie-Moo!" said Kat. "You are so sweet."

"Just because *they* all bonded at uni, there's no reason that we should all get on in the same way, is there?" said Jem. "No reason at all."

"But we do," I said, looking over at Kat to back me up.

She said nothing and carried on smoothing cream into her face. "My dad and his midlife crisis have done their best to trash it anyway."

"We've got our trip to Greece after my A-levels," I said. "We can look forward to that."

She didn't answer because Dom had wandered out of the kitchen with an espresso cup and an unlit cigarette dangling from his fingers.

"Another day in paradise. Cool." He sat on the edge of the last sun lounger and drained his coffee. He wore pink shorts, a navy polo shirt and deck shoes. His sunglasses were so dark I couldn't see where he was looking.

But I could guess.

"Ah. Staying here would be so much more fun than going sailing." He reached over Kat to take the sun-cream bottle. "A *much* better view."

I thought she'd have some smart remark to make. But she didn't. She laughed. A silly tinkle of a giggle.

I pulled my towel over me like a sheet, right up to my chin.

"I do believe you've missed a bit," said Dom and leaned towards Kat's face. He tapped the tip of her nose with a blob of lotion. "Right here."

A horn sounded – Nick's car. Dom unfurled his body and slowly stood up, sighing deeply. "Ah well. No rest for the wicked."

He lit his cigarette and inhaled before passing it to Kat. They held each other's gaze as her lips closed around it. The horn sounded again. "I'll see you ladies later. Be careful you don't get burnt." He whistled as he walked slowly away round the side of the house and we heard the car drive off on the gravel.

"He was practically drooling," said Jem. "Your mum would go ballistic. And as for your dad, does he know what a tool Dom is?"

"He's not," said Kat. "He's way better than Tim the sweaty accountant from New Year. Remember him? And my father doesn't get to have an opinion on anything now. Dom's actually OK once you get to know him. Generous.

Doesn't mean he'll last, though." She adjusted her bikini straps.

"And have you, got to *know* him?" said Jem, leaning up on one elbow and flicking my book at Kat. "Honestly, Kat. Why do you have to push everything?"

Kat picked up her phone and earbuds. "I think it's going to be a beautiful day, don't you?" she said. She tucked the buds into her ears and lay back with her eyes closed. She took another puff on the cigarette. A small smile flickered across her lips. If I didn't know her so well, I might have missed it.

Dear Kat,

Secrets are a burden.

I used to want to be the keeper of your secrets. I was honoured to be within the Kat inner circle of trust. I'd wanted it for long enough. I keep my promises, cross my heart and hope to die.

But, you see, back then I didn't know.

I didn't know about the burden part being heavier than the gift. I didn't know about the cost.

Everything always has a cost with you.

Lots of love,

Millie xx

10 August 2019
Missing: 363 days

We spend what's left of the morning in the garden or down on the river beach. Taking turns on the paddleboards, sunbathing, lazing. If you describe it like that, it sounds idyllic. *Elysian* is my new word for it.

But it isn't. Not for me.

We all tread on eggshells around Charlie – as though he's the one who misses Kat most, who's suffered most. No one, not one of them, asks *me* how *I*'m feeling, if I'm OK. And it's dawning on me that the new incarnation of 'the Girls' means me and Jem and that what she said last year was true: the fact our mothers became instant friends during freshers' week nearly thirty years ago does NOT mean that their daughters will be BFFs age sixteen and seventeen. Sure, we had a mutual love of cuddly-toy tea parties age three and four; the Hungry Hippos game age six and seven; and a Cluedo craze age twelve and thirteen; but spending time together now is harder. Me and Jem don't like the same books or music, we go to very different schools, enjoy different subjects, have zero mutual friends to talk about. Once she goes off to uni and pursues her great legal career, I doubt we'll even see each other again. She doesn't share anything important with me; she holds back on what she says. And I tell her nothing more personal than what subjects I'm doing for A-level next term.

By two o'clock, we're all hungry, though too lazy to sort

anything out to eat. "Shall we put together a picnic to take back down to the water?" I suggest.

"A picnic? With our ickle teddy bears?" mocks Matt. "Er, no. Not when there's a perfectly good pub within walking distance serving chips."

"And real ale," says Charlie, brightening up at the prospect.

Jem yawns and says: "Happy to go with the flow."

"Sea Trout Inn it is, then," says Matt, rubbing his hands together.

*

The pub is the stupid idea I knew it would be. The garden's rammed on a sunny August Saturday and we end up perched on the edge of a picnic table in the garden, sharing with a couple of pensioners and their dog who 'is being friendly' by alternately humping any unattended lower leg or snarling at us.

Matt, as the only one with ID, gets the drinks in. There are a few stares and whispers as he carries the tray over.

"Do they know who we are?" I whisper to Jem.

"Course not. Ignore it."

"We're allowed to go out and enjoy ourselves," says Matt.

The boys mess about flipping beer mats and talk about Matt's party plans with his school friends for A-level results day on Thursday. Matt's being dizzyingly cheerful and it's giving me a headache. I wish everyone would stop pretending this is normal. This is not normal. And if he's still meant to be keeping Charlie away from alcohol, he's failing badly – Charlie's on his second pint before the food even arrives.

A couple of men sit down at the next table. They're talking to each other in low voices and staring over at us. I could pretend it's because I'm irresistibly gorgeous, but I know that isn't true. And Jem's got her back to them so it can't be her actual gorgeousness. It could be that Charlie is their type, but I don't think it's that either. Charlie's leg is rammed in next to mine and he starts jigging it in agitation. "Got a problem?" His voice is loud and sharp.

"You're the twin, aren't you? Of that girl?" says one. "Looks like you're having a jolly holiday."

Charlie's up and lunging at them, his legs tangling with the bench in his haste. He aims a punch at the shorter one who's too slow to get out of the way, or too shocked. Their drinks spill across the table and the beer pours through the slatted gaps. The taller one grabs at Charlie's collar and pulls him back and down so his face smashes into the table. He's bleeding from the bridge of his nose. It's Jem rather than Matt who's there first, apologizing profusely for Charlie and pushing herself between the guys as she helps Charlie up.

The waitress stands transfixed with a tray of burgers before retreating back into the pub. Matt's trying to talk

Charlie down while the guys are mouthing off at him.

"You've broken my sunglasses," says the short one. "And cut my nose."

I stare at the last of the beer trickling on to the ground as the annoying dog yaps and yaps. We should never have come here.

Noah arrives wearing a pub T-shirt and holding a tea towel. Like that's going to help.

"All right? What's the problem, lads?"

"This stuck-up dick punched us," says the tall one.

"For no reason?" says Noah. "What did you do, Luke?"

"Stay out of it, Biscoe," says the shorter one, with his face tipped up to stop his nose bleeding. "I should be able to get a drink here without being decked by the emmets or the incomers. No one in a family like yours gets to tell me what to do – not your dad or your lying cousin, and not you."

"My friend is sorry," says Matt. "Aren't you, Charlie, mate? His sister is a sensitive topic."

"We thought you lot had pissed off back to London for good," Luke says, dabbing at the spilled beer on his shorts. "Your family's caused no end of trouble for this village."

"What, because his sister disappeared? You're all heart, aren't you?" says Jem, looking like she might hit them next.

The dog is barking louder and louder and I need to get out of here.

"Let's all calm down a bit," says Noah.

"Why are you even here? What's it got to do with you?

114

What's my sister got to do with you?" says Charlie, about an inch from Noah's face, until Matt pulls him back.

I stand up. "I'll pay for your drinks that got knocked over." Dad gave me emergency money. I'm not sure that paying off a couple of guys Charlie's got into a fight with was exactly the emergency he had in mind, but too bad. I put £20 on the wet table. "Let's go, please." I tug at Matt's sleeve.

"You can stick your crappy pub, the lot of you," shouts Charlie, as Matt's trying to steer him back towards the path. "Don't ever mention my sister again, any of you." He stumbles backwards slightly as he sweeps his arm across the whole pub garden. Making sure he's left no one out of his rant. Turns out this really will be our last ever trip to the Sea Trout Inn.

Jem hurries after the boys.

"I'm sorry," I say. To Noah, to the two guys, to the pensioners at the table, to the whole pub garden. Even to the angry dog. To everyone.

"I'm so sorry."

7 August 2018

Charlie and Matt's room smelled of them. Their sports socks and shirts were in a heap by the door. Canisters of cheap deodorant were scattered on the windowsill. I sniffed each one to work out whose was whose. Name That Armpit. A new game. Too easy. I moved the bookmark forward a chapter in Matt's book. Charlie had a football magazine next to his bed and a mess of used cups and glasses. If there had been a little something I wanted, I'd have taken it. Honestly, though, I didn't want anything from there.

But enough frivolity, I was there to suss out any new hiding places. No one was keen on playing hide-and-seek yet, but I had days to work on them before the last-night party. If it was raining, we'd hide indoors like at New Year and I could do with some new spots to use.

The boys' bedroom has three hiding places we used when we were little: under the beds; the trunk by the window which we've all outgrown now; and the wardrobe alcove next to the fireplace. I crouched to look under their beds. Used tissues and discarded footwear. Unappealing.

I tried the alcove with its hanging rail and stripey curtain. I could still squeeze in despite the empty suitcases and hanging clothes. But it would be too tight for the boys. I was pleased to have found somewhere I could keep on the list, even if it wouldn't be that comfortable for long. But then I heard voices on the landing and Matt and Kat came into the bedroom. I sank down, holding the ill-fitting curtain closed.

They were meant to be out. Matt was supposed to be walking somewhere and Kat was kayaking along the creek. Why weren't they saying anything? Kat was squealing and giggling and then all I could hear was rustling and heavy breathing. I peeped through a tiny gap but the slurpy sound effects were already telling me exactly what they were doing.

And it was revolting.

They were Creekers – they shouldn't have been doing it. We'd known each other for forever. We were like family. *Family*. This would ruin everything.

It was too confusing. Matt and Kat had practically ignored each other since I'd been here. And hadn't she hinted that Dom had given her the ridiculously tiny bikini? *This* wasn't possible. I made a wider chink and looked again. Matt was up against the closed door and they were kissing each other. Kat's skirt had ridden up and he ran his hands up and down her thighs and bottom. He was groping her and she was letting him. She was unbuckling his belt.

I snapped my eyes shut. But had to open them again. Kat was moaning and writhing against him, but Matt had stopped touching her, his hands hovering in mid-air to each side of her. He was stretching his neck away.

"Kat, no. We agreed," he said, squeezing out from against the door and backing off across the room. "It was a one-off,

117

nothing. We agreed. You and me is not a good idea."

Finally. At least one of them was seeing sense.

"It *felt* like you thought it was a good idea just now," she said, moving towards him. She pushed him back gently on to the bed. "Everyone's out. How often does that happen here? No one's watching us for once."

Matt laughed nervously. "We should quit while we're ahead. Before it gets out of hand." He started to sit up, but she gently pushed him back. "You realize we cannot be a couple – our names rhyme. Matt/Kat. Kat/Matt. Either way, sounds stupid."

"The Kat sat on the Matt." She shuffled forward on the bed to sit astride him, her hair tumbling into his face. She took his arms and pinned them above his head. "I could get used to it," she said.

I flexed my toes. Cramp was crawling up my left leg.

"Kat, seriously. Charlie might come back early."

"So?" She kissed the side of his neck.

"I don't think he'd like me and you, you know…"

"And I don't care what my brother thinks. He'd be way more protective of you and your bromance than bothered about what his twin gets up to anyway."

Matt shifted away from under her and stood up. "Stop, Kat. It's not going to happen." His voice was sharper, no longer jokey. "Take the hint."

I bit my lip. A wave of Kat's humiliation crashed through the room. The bed creaked as she got up and rebuttoned her top before brushing down her clothes.

"Kat, we don't need to fall out over this."

"Of course not. Because it was nothing. Isn't that what you said? Nothing. You're right – you're way too immature for me."

"You won't tell Charlie, will you? Are we cool?"

She waited a moment. "Very cool," she said with a voice that could carve an ice sculpture.

"Seriously, Kat, don't speak to Charlie. Kat?"

Kat moved out of my line of vision and the door slammed. Matt swore and kicked out at the bed.

The cramp was getting worse. I moved slightly to stretch my leg, which knocked the clothes so that the coat hangers jangled. I closed my eyes tight shut.

Matt pulled back the curtain. "Shit, Millie. How long have you been there?"

"I … I must have nodded off." Both of us were turning assorted shades of beetroot red.

"What the hell are you doing hiding in our room? Did Kat put you up to it?"

"No!" I hopped awkwardly from leg to leg. "I was checking out new hiding places for the game."

"You're always watching, always hiding. It's creepy."

"I didn't see anything," I stuttered. "If there was anything to see, I mean."

"Yeah, sure. I believe you."

"I won't say a word, I swear. I closed my eyes – I fell asleep

119

and then it was too late to leave. I didn't see anything."

"Who were you watching most through your little peepy-hole, Millie? Me or Kat?"

I didn't answer.

Matt sighed. "Let me give you some advice. Hiding from everyone and everything won't stop you getting hurt. Especially by Kat."

Dear Kat,

The others aren't as into playing games as you and me.

I know that not everyone gets it.

It seems to me that how you play a board game is how you go through life.

Some players want to read every line of the rules and plan ahead before they take a single throw of the dice.

Some wing it and pick it up as they go along.

Others turn the board up when it's not going their way and ruin it for everyone.

Some are the kind of player who move the meeples when no one's watching. And I reckon that's what you like to do, Kat – to move the players round the board, manipulate everyone exactly where you want them to be so that you get to win the game.

Just a theory,

Love,

Millie xxx

10 August 2019
Missing: 363 days

When I answer the doorbell, I find Noah standing on the doorstep. He's brought over the stuff we left at the pub after making a hasty exit – Matt's sweatshirt and Jem's sunhat. "I wanted to check you were all OK," he says.

"We're fine. Charlie's had a frozen bag of peas on his knuckles and we sorted the cuts on his face. We were stupid to go to the village pub."

"This whole area survives on tourism. What happened last summer is a very touchy subject."

What does he think it's like for us, for me?

His eyes flicker down the hall.

"Charlie didn't mean all that stuff he said," I lie. "Come on in." I take the hat and sweatshirt and lead him down the hallway. Matt and Charlie have flopped on to the sofas in the TV room and are engrossed in their phones.

"Noah brought our things back from the pub," I say.

Charlie grunts, not raising his eyes.

"You didn't need to," says Matt.

Jem fiddles with the clasp on her bracelet. "Ignore them. Their testosterone is still calming down. Thanks." She smiles weakly.

"It was Noah and his mum who opened up the house for us," I say trying to change the atmosphere. "And filled up the fridge."

"I know. Anna and Nick pay them to," says Charlie, looking up and fixing his gaze on Noah long enough to make him uncomfortable.

I should call him out. I should tell him not to be so foul. But I don't. I lead Noah into the kitchen. "Please thank your mum for doing the flowers," I say.

"Sure." He looks down at his feet. "Actually, it was me. Not bad for my first go at flower arranging. Mum asked me to sort the house and food and everything. Her back's bad again."

He turns to the sink and loads up the dirty serving bowls from last night which we'd dumped on the side. "I'll wash these up and then I can take them back with me."

"If you're sure." I'm awkward watching him. It was OK to have his mum pottering around when we were all here in the holidays, clearing up after everyone, and taking instructions from Anna and Nick, but he's only three years older than me. "The food was great. Thanks. There's another dish knocking around somewhere – I'll get it."

I take my time so I'm saved any more small talk. I pick up the last of the dirty plates and glasses from the TV room. Charlie doesn't even look up.

"Why do you have to be so rude to Noah? He stuck up for you at the pub."

"Shoot me for not laying out the red carpet for the guy who was shagging my sister before she disappeared," says Charlie. "You do know that, right?"

My stomach flips. "She ... he wouldn't have," I say.

"Oh, grow up, Mills."

"She'd have told me."

"There's plenty my sister didn't tell people, including you."

"That's not true."

"And don't start inviting him over to the house. He was questioned by the police. They thought he might have had something to do with Kat going missing."

"Keep your voice down. He's in the kitchen," I say. "Jem and Matt's family has known him and his mum for years. And the police didn't charge him with anything. He wasn't even in the area."

"Don't act like we grew up with the guy," says Matt.

"And we're here for a couple of weeks every year," says Charlie. "None of us really know him. He's not one of us."

"A Creeker?"

"No one's used that term since we were ten, Millie. He's not, you know, like us."

Matt tosses his phone on to the sofa. "Charlie's right. We've barely spoken to him since we were tiny kids and he came with his mum sometimes, maybe the odd chat at the pub. He only started hanging around in the last year or so – ogling Kat and Jem probably. That's it."

"See," says Charlie. "Don't get all buddy-buddy with him, Millie."

When I get back to the kitchen, Noah's stacking the cool

bag with the clean dishes. I'd know deep down if he was any danger, right? Murderers don't tidy up your kitchen and do your washing-up.

"I should go," he says. "I get the impression Kat's brother's not very happy to see me."

"It's fine," I say, but even I don't believe my tone. "Charlie's in a difficult place right now," I add, parroting what Mum tried to tell me before I left. "After all that's happened." There I go again with the euphemisms.

"Yeah, I get it." Noah picks up the bag. "I've got to go anyway. Another shift at the pub tonight. I shouldn't be late." He heads towards the kitchen door with a half wave. I know he couldn't have had anything to do with Kat's disappearance that night. Could he? He's nice and kind and tries to stop people being punched in the face and arranges flowers in vases. He wasn't shagging Kat.

As I turn to go and join the others, I notice his black jacket's hanging off the back of one of the chairs. I call out to him.

He stops.

"You've…" I begin. But then I remember that's where his key to the boathouse is – tucked inside the zip pocket of his jacket. And the key is my way to see exactly what he didn't want to show me this morning. To put my mind at rest about him.

"You've been such a help today. Thank you," I finish, and I flash the Kat smile that I've been trying out for size recently. The insincere one, but the one that always seemed to work.

"Sure. No worries," he says and nods. "See you around?"

"Definitely," I say, too chicken to tell him the boys want him around here as little as possible. And I watch his back disappear round the corner of the house towards the drive.

As soon as he's out of sight, I pick up his jacket and take the key, shoving it quickly into my own pocket. Jem comes in before I've put the jacket back down and it looks like I'm cuddling it. That and the guilty look on my face lead her to crack up laughing. "No way, Millie! You and Noah. You don't waste any time, do you! Even after what Charlie said. I didn't think he was your type, but you go, girl."

The heat spreads across my face as I flounder. "I'm not… I mean, no."

"Your secret's safe with me, Mills," she says with a smirk that says as soon as my back's turned, she'll tell Matt and Charlie. "Kat will be a hard act to follow, though. For anyone," she says. Her eyes linger a little too long looking me up and down and I know she's thinking that I am so not in Kat's league.

But I know that already.

Dear Kat,

Today I was told something new about you. I thought I knew most things but turns out you still have secrets tucked away. It makes me think.

It makes me think what else you lied about, and how many things I don't know about you. That you didn't share with me, your very best friend.

Millie xxx

8 August 2018

"We should go to the beach today," said Matt. "Take the boards. I checked my phone and the surf's good. And there's a beach party later with a barbecue and fireworks. I could ask Dad to lend us the car."

"There's no way he's going to let you after you scratched it in the car park," said Jem.

"That was not my fault. Those bollards were too close together."

"I'm OK staying here," I said. "We could go for a walk down to the village."

Matt sighed. "Millie. We all know you'd be happy staying within a two-mile radius of Creek House and never leaving it, but the rest of us like to live a little. You and Kat could stay here." Matt paused taking the mickey out of me to see what vehicle was screeching up to the house and gave a low whistle. I joined him at the landing window. It was a car we knew well but hadn't seen for a while. A white Porsche Cayenne with a personalised number plate: ROB 001. And a furious-looking Rob got out. The car windows were tinted but not so much that we couldn't see a dark-haired woman in the front seat.

"Pull up a chair," said Matt. "Our day is about to get interesting."

"Where's Kat and Charlie?" I asked.

"Maybe it's best they don't know," said Jem. "Kat's

upstairs drying her hair."

"Charlie's out with the kayak," said Matt. "Thank God I didn't go with him. I wouldn't want to miss this for anything."

"We shouldn't eavesdrop," I said.

"Are you *insane*? Of course we should," said Matt, pushing me further along the windowsill and opening up the window wider. "This is going to be awesome."

We had an excellent view of Rob's bald patch as he rang the doorbell in an angry set of three rings.

"Is the au pair going to get out of the car?" whispered Matt.

"She has a name," I said. "Giselle. She has a degree in history."

"I don't think Rob was interested in her history degree," said Matt.

"Shut up," said Jem. "And this isn't a show for your entertainment." She was much less enthusiastic than I thought she'd be.

"You shush," said Matt. "We're missing it."

Rob's voice floated up. Posh and clipped. Followed by the familiar sound of Liz's voice, though hers had moved up an octave. "Have you driven down all this way to shout at me?"

"Don't flatter yourself. We're having a few days away. And I've been more than tolerant with you."

Jem leaned further forward on the windowsill and accidentally knocked over a vase. Matt and I both reached to catch it and fumbled but it didn't break.

"Quiet or they'll know we're watching," said Matt. "Why do you have to be so clumsy?"

Liz was getting angrier and angrier. She rammed her finger hard into Rob's chest. "Tolerant? What the hell are you talking about?"

"Don't play the innocent. It stops. Now."

"If this is about the credit card…"

"I've cancelled that. I'm not funding you, your Botox, your handbags, your yoga classes. I've tried to do this in an amicable way but *you* plainly can't."

Anna arrived, pushing Nick in front of her. He still had a phone clamped to his chest. Nick reached out a hand. "Look, buddy, let's take this down a notch."

"Buddy? You're not my buddy. You've all taken HER side in this – if you even knew what she's like. And as for Brodie, that so-called friend, he's in a class of his own…"

"Why's he laying into my dad too?" I whispered, as Mum rocked up to join the party, nervously wiping her hands on the tea towel she was still clutching.

"Shh," said Matt. "This is getting interesting."

"You see what I have to contend with," said Liz, turning back towards Anna and Mum.

"I haven't even started yet," said Rob.

"I think you're about finished here," said Nick. He was broad and taller than Rob. And now he looked like someone who'd throw a punch if he had to. Even if that someone was his oldest friend. Ex-friend. Rob was right that everyone had taken sides in this. We'd all picked teams, exactly like in the old annual rounders match, except Rob and Giselle had ended up in a team of two at the far end of the field.

Dom was nowhere to be seen. The floorboards creaked along the hall. The coward was keeping a low profile in his and Liz's room. Unlike mine and Kat's, their room was at the front of the house so there was no way he wasn't aware of this. I guess standing up for Liz against estranged husbands wasn't on his holiday wish list.

The passenger car door opened and a pair of pink pumps hit the ground.

"Uh-oh," said Matt. "Wait for the biggest explosion of all."

Giselle used the top of the door to help herself out of the car – and once she'd done so we all understood why she'd had to heave herself out of the vehicle. She had the biggest baby bump I'd ever seen.

She cupped her hands around the top and bottom of her tummy which made it seem even bigger and rounder as her dress stretched across it.

Like a giant, ripe, fertile watermelon.

We all leaned out further to look at Liz by the front door. She stepped back against the door frame. Nick's face was a picture too.

"Oh my good God," said Jem. "She's pregnant."

"Nothing gets past you, Jem," said her brother, nudging

her elbow.

She slumped down and sat on the floor, her suntanned face looking suddenly pale.

"Rob, honey. I have to use the loo!" called Giselle.

"She can't use the one here!" said Liz.

"You're seriously saying she has to wait until we get to the hotel?" said Rob.

"Hotel? Expensive one, is it? I expect they have very nice restrooms. Or the local Esso garage has one at the back of the shop if she can't wait."

"You're being ridiculous."

"I'm not the ridiculous one in this scenario," screamed Liz. "Of all the places for you to go on holiday, why did you have to come down here?"

"In case you hadn't noticed, we can't get on a plane at the moment. And you don't own the whole of bloody Cornwall."

Giselle had begun her slow waddle towards the front door but Liz showed no sign of moving.

"Who's going to tell Kat?" I said in a whisper.

"Tell me what?" Kat stood behind us in her cotton dressing gown, brushing out her hair. She looked from me to Matt to Jem and pulled Matt out of the way. She leaned out of the window next to me and looked at the scene below laid out like a stage. We had the best seats in the house. She let out a yelp and the players all turned and looked up at the two of us.

She ran down the stairs and burst through the front door like an avenging angel with her hair and gown billowing around her as she ran up to her father, stopped right in front of him and slapped him hard in the face. The sound of flesh on flesh made me wince. It echoed around the driveway.

Giselle gasped and began to cry. "You!" she sobbed. "How could you?"

Kat stood there shaking with rage. Liz wrapped her arms around her and pulled her back. Rob said nothing. Not in actual words. He put his hand up to his face and rubbed the spot where she'd hit him. He turned the sobbing Giselle around and helped her back into the car. He shut her door carefully before getting in himself without a backward glance.

"Daddy," screamed Kat. "Daddy!" She shook off Liz, ran towards the car and yanked at his door handle as he reversed.

Liz pulled her back again, holding her tight while Rob, Giselle and the belly drove off.

"Holy cow," said Matt. "I did say I wanted fireworks."

Dear Kat,

Adults don't have all the answers.

They make the problems, but they don't have all the answers.

Millie xx

I hurry back down to Tide Beach before I can chicken out. I want Noah's secrecy to be nothing to do with me or Kat but I have to make sure. At the boathouse I fumble with the key and the door sticks so I lean my shoulder against it to give it a final shove.

Noah should be working at the pub right now. But I can't say for sure how long I've got before he realizes he left his jacket and key at Creek House and comes back for it. Until later tonight? Tomorrow? The light's starting to fail. I need to do this and head back before the others wonder where I am.

I step into the gloom and switch on my phone light. The long, thin rowing boat is moored in the water, which laps gently against its sides. I tread carefully on the slippery stones to reach the wooden door and the stairs up to the mezzanine. I flick the light around the upper floor. He's got a couple of chairs, a khaki camp bed with a pillow and a rolled-up sleeping bag. There's a table with a small stove and a kettle. A battered tin tray holds tea and coffee and a few old mugs. Most of them dirty.

When I raise the phone and take in the rest of the place, I gasp. A rectangle has been marked out on the wooden wall above the camp bed, about two metres by one metre. And it's like a true-crime documentary in here because it's covered with bits of paper and photos and felt-tip arrows and lengths of tape linking them all together. A map of this area is pinned up on the adjoining wall, with tiny pin flags and routes marked in red. Stuck all over the place are photos of Kat – ones I know from her social media, but others too, taken here – Kat in the white bikini, Kat paddling at the edge of the water. Kat on the paddleboard. A whole photo essay of last summer.

But she's not looking at the camera in all of them. In some she's not posing and pouting like she usually did for a photo.

She's not looking at the camera because she didn't know the photos were being taken.

There's another board to the right with pictures of the rest of the Creekers. All of us laid out. I move the light from me to Charlie to Matt to Jem. Noah knew my name all right – he's written it up in felt tip under my photo. There's a picture of Liz cut out from the local paper – *Desperate mother in plea for information on her missing daughter* and lines leading from her to Rob and Dom.

As I start to read the Post-it notes and try to make sense of what's scribbled on them, the stairs creak and I quickly switch off my light.

I duck down behind a chair, knocking the tea tray. To my horror, the jar of coffee rumbles across the floor and comes to rest with a final smack against the wall. Loud. Stupid, stupid me – my last thought before the feet on the stairs reach the gallery.

"I know you're there. Come out before you break anything." Noah's voice fills the space. He turns on two large, battery-operated lanterns which cast long shadows on the walls, picking out parts of his incident board.

I rise slowly from behind the chair, though he could clearly see me before.

"What is it with you lot and hiding?" he says sharply. He picks up the coffee jar and sets it back on the tin tray.

"You dropped your key up at Creek House so I thought I'd return it," I say, struggling to think of a good excuse for my being in here, breaking in without permission.

"By letting yourself in with it? Checking it worked?" He shakes his head and mutters "Unbelievable!" under his breath.

"I really wanted to see the renovations. I … I didn't know all this was here."

"Come on in! Help yourself!" he says, gesturing round the room. "Because what any of you lot want, you always get."

"I should have asked. I'm sorry," I say. "Do you want me to go?"

"I suppose you're here now. What have you touched?"

"Nothing, honestly."

He pours water from a large plastic container into the kettle and lights the camp stove. The gas hisses to fill the silence. He slowly makes us hot drinks. All while keeping half an eye on me. He never even glances at the stonking great elephant in the room – his very own serial-killer wall displays.

It's not until I'm clasping a mug of black coffee with both hands, and have burned my tongue taking a nervous sip, that he finally gestures at it all.

"I guess you want to know why this is here?" he says.

"It's your boathouse," I say. Part of me wants to apologize again and offer to go. But the part that wants an explanation wins. "But what the heck is this, Noah?"

"Luke at the pub had a point today – you people do come here and wreck everything. You breeze in and out. I got hauled in and questioned over Kat. I lost my job at the shop over it."

"We all got questioned, Noah."

"You lot got questioned as witnesses, not as suspects. Not by someone asking you every personal detail of your life, your intimate life. Did you get treated like a criminal?"

I shake my head. None of the Creekers had.

"Until they find Kat alive and well or find Kat's body..." he says.

I flinch, but he breezes on as though she's not important in this. As though it's about him.

"...and decide she took her own life or arrest someone else, some people are always going to think I had something to do with it." He packs away the stove and matches. "You know what people say down here?"

136

"No smoke without fire," I say with a weak smile.

But he doesn't laugh. "They say bad will out. That my dad was no good, so I'm no good too. He's been in and out of trouble all his life – that's why my mum booted him out long ago. Do you know how hard Mum and I have tried to shake all that off? Only to be told it's all in the genes and my dad's a loser so I must be too."

"That's not true. That's not fair."

"If they hadn't sacked me at the shop, I'd probably have left anyway. Parents were saying they didn't want their kids to go in there if I was working." He frowns. "My babysitting jobs certainly dried up. All that mud sticks. It's taken me and Mum months to persuade the pub to take me on – out the back in the kitchen – but it's better than nothing. And then Charlie had to go and do *that* today. Ali the landlord cancelled my shift tonight."

"You just have to explain. I could get Charlie to say something."

"Beginning to see how the world works for normal people outside your rich bubble of second homes and fancy schools?"

"My family aren't…"

"I don't even take photos any more – used to mean I was creative, artistic. Now it makes me creepy, makes me look like a peeping Tom." He stands by the photos and looks hard at them. "Kat liked my photos – or said she did. I showed her the ones I'd taken of objects washed up by the tide for my BTEC. She said I should sell them at the tourist galleries."

Maybe I need to see them because right now the ones of Kat pinned up here in secret look more creepy than artistic.

"She said she'd take some to show to the professional photographer who was staying with you – Dom Crawford. Said they were like ones at an exhibition they'd been to in Bristol. But she never did."

Dom Crawford. I never even knew Dom's surname. Noah has stuck up a print from a website homepage – full of arty shots of landscapes. Sounds like he and Kat were going places together at home, *before* the holiday. With her mum, or without? I didn't know about that.

I unpin a newspaper article and skim-read it. It's one from the *Cornish Herald* last September: *Local boy questioned again over missing girlfriend.*

"All that stuff in there," he says. "It's not true. I wasn't even here that night she went missing. You know that. I was up country in Exeter with my cousin – but they don't bother pointing that out in the paper." He snorts. "Girlfriend! In my dreams. We weren't ever going out together. A couple of kisses, a hand up her top…"

I redden. I don't want to hear this. The comment from one of his neighbours leaps out at me from the paper: "*Noah Biscoe's always been a misfit. A loner.*"

"We didn't ever … you know."

I nod, still blushing. I *knew* she'd have told me.

"It was something and nothing," he says, rubbing at his temples. "She was playing me somehow, stringing me along, but I couldn't see why. No way someone that beautiful would be interested in me. I was an idiot to believe it for a short while. And now I'm stuck with this bloody great cloud over me."

I'm uncomfortable being his support buddy. Even though I've got lifetime membership of the misfit club. "I'm sorry. I didn't think…"

"That's the difference between your life and mine. You lot don't have to think about anything. At least I'll get some work with the next people doing up Creek House. They don't know yet I'm 'the local loner'." He jabs his finger bitterly at the article.

"*I* don't think you had anything to do with what happened to Kat."

"Yeah, but Charlie does, right?" He clears away our mugs. "I suppose you can't think I'm involved. Because here you are, all alone with me, the potential attacker. And nobody knows where you are." He waggles his fingers and makes a spooky 'oooh' noise.

My lips turn dry and I swallow hard. Mum and Dad would freak out at me creeping around the place where Kat disappeared, being alone with one of the people who was questioned about her. And this whole set-up looks so weird. Obsessional. Murderers keep trophies of the people they kill, or hang around the investigation. This could all be some giant souvenir or token.

But I know Noah had nothing to do with Kat's disappearance that night. Both my heart and my head are telling me that.

"You had an alibi," I say. "And no motive."

"Thanks, Miss Marple. You don't buy the dumped boyfriend theory that police officer had?"

"Honestly, I don't think a one-off fondle meant anything much to either of you. For Kat, well, it meant nothing." He flinches slightly.

"You know…" He pauses and seems like he's weighing up whether to say something. "You know there's been activity on her Instagram account recently? Pics have been posted. I told the police about it but didn't hear anything back. They were probably more concerned that I'd been keeping an eye on her social media accounts." His face settles into a scowl again. "People see what they want to see, twist everything to fit their set of facts."

I pull up Kat's Instagram account: @Livresque_KB. He's right – there are two new posts in the last week. I fumble as I scrutinize the pictures: one of a beach #LivingtheDream #GreatEscapes and one of a cocktail on a bar #KatsGotTheCream.

"Do you think it's her?" I ask.

"I've studied those pictures again and again. A tiny bit of a foot is shown on the beach shot. You look. You knew her. Is that her foot?"

He stands close as I study my screen, his warm breath hitting my cheek.

I zoom in on the image. The glimpse of flesh isn't enough to tell. It could be any white girl on a sandy beach. It could be me.

"We talked about going to Greece one day," I say. "Together. Island hopping. Going to that place in the *Mamma Mia* films. Could it be there?"

"Like I'd know," he says. "And when there's a picture, it doesn't mean it's taken in real time. It could be a stock photo."

There's a fluttering in my chest at the idea of Kat being out there sipping this cocktail and lounging on a beautiful beach. Even though I know it's not her usual kind of picture – she's not in it, centre stage.

"Someone else with access could have posted it, or hacked the account," he says. "She could have scheduled the post herself."

Whatever, it makes me think, it makes me *hope*, that she's still out there, posting pictures. I tuck my phone back in my pocket.

"One-year anniversary coming up," says Noah. "Maybe that's why."

I nod, annoyed that Noah who meant nothing to her has spotted these pictures. "Her mum has had all kinds of trolling – letters pretending to be from her, messages on social media saying terrible things. She's even had a woman on the doorstep saying the spirits had told her where Kat was."

A psychic kept hounding Liz until she agreed to a session – for £500 – and a load of upsetting hocus pocus about the smell of jasmine perfume and Kat needing her help. Mum put a stop to it before Liz did another session. Liz must have known it was all rubbish but she wanted to do it. She'd have paid double the fee. Another straw to grasp at.

I go back to the giant board. A photo of Kat catches my eye and I can't pull myself away from it. From her.

Noah stands beside me, looking at the wall. He sighs. "I thought if I could find out what really happened to her, I could move on with my life."

"Me too. But the others don't – they think it's pointless, hopeless to even try."

Noah's like me. Like Charlie. Stuck in a place he doesn't want to be until Kat comes home. *If* Kat comes home.

"Perhaps they're right. I've certainly hit a dead end," he says. "Maybe it's a good thing you've seen it and not freaked out."

Oh, I've freaked out all right. On the inside.

He clears his throat. "You could see what you think of what I've put together. It might make more sense to you. Help me join some dots, fill in the gaps. If you want to – I know you're not here for long."

Maybe I should at least find out what he knows about all of us, what secrets he's unearthed. Even if we can't find out what happened to Kat, I want to get her pictures down off this wall. She's being picked apart by someone who barely knew her.

"I'm leaving on Monday morning but if you think I can help, I could come again tomorrow," I say. "Best not say anything to the others." Not least because after what Charlie said about Noah today, and the way he's been lately, that could be a majorly bad idea.

"I warn you," says Noah, as he locks up the boatshed as we leave, "you might not like what we find out."

Dear Kat,

I don't know why you treated Noah so badly except that it reflects your general patterns of behaviour.

You hurt him.

But then you hurt everybody.

Millie x

8 August 2018

The day was ruined. I sat with my book on the low branch in the yew hollow. I'd borrowed it from Kat and wanted to finish it quickly so we could talk about it, calm her down, have a conversation the other Creekers wouldn't muscle in on. She only discussed books with me.

It was good to have some space from them all for a while. Mum and Anna had taken Liz out to a seaside bar she liked so she could vent without Kat and Charlie hearing.

There was too much noise and anger and upset floating round. I wanted it to be like last year with the biggest row being over a game of Twister or swingball. That's how I remembered it. Pretend anger, jesting anger. Not this.

A door to the house slammed. Charlie was walking across the lawn in his swim shorts and sliders with a towel over his shoulder. Kat was running after him calling his name. "Hold up, Charlie. I want to speak to you."

Charlie stopped by the yew, turned and sighed. "You've said enough already."

"I haven't even started," said Kat, her hands on her hips. I didn't need to see her face clearly to know she was still livid.

I adjusted how I was sitting on the branch to edge closer. Charlie was speaking quietly compared to Kat's outbursts. I could only see glimpses of them as they moved – a flash of Kat's purple shirt here and there.

"What's happened between Mum and Dad, don't let that

ruin things between us and Dad," said Charlie.

"I might have known you'd be on his side. Have you been in touch with him all this time?"

"Kind of, yes."

"When did you know about the baby?"

"You saw Giselle – it's kind of hard not to notice, even for me. But they told me a few months ago."

"And you didn't say anything to me and Mum!"

"It's not my news to tell. They were waiting for the right time, I guess."

"The right time? Today was not the right time."

"Agreed. But it's better out in the open now."

"So you don't have to be a lying, sneaking snake."

"Firstly, it was up to them whether to tell you and, secondly, I was worried you'd go ballistic. And it turns out I was right on that one. For your information, Giselle's really upset about how it's all worked out," said Charlie. "She's actually very sweet and she's had a tough time of it too. Her life isn't all rainbows and unicorns."

"Quick, find me a tiny violin for the home-wrecker."

"Dad and Mum were falling apart without Giselle. Give her a break."

"Oh my God. That's it, isn't it. I've been an idiot. *You* fancy her too. Did you fancy her when she was babysitting and tucking you up in bed in your spaceman pyjamas or is this a recent thing?"

"Don't be stupid. That's sick." Charlie sighed again and I

caught a glimpse of him reaching out to touch her but she pushed his arm away. "Dad and Giselle love each other, Kat. And that baby is going to be our little brother or sister."

"Half-brother or half-sister. I don't want to see it, ever. You realize he'll dump us once he's got a new baby to coo over and pay for. He's already said he's cutting back on school fees."

"He wants to see us. Both of us."

"What about Mum? Have you got no loyalty to Mum?"

"Kat. This isn't a Disney movie – there's no way Mum and Dad are ever getting back together. Too much has happened. Blimey, we've had to put up with Dom this week and him and Mum pawing each other. You can't blame Giselle for all that and you can't blame a tiny baby."

He turned to go. "I need a swim. I'm sick of you, Katherine. Everything has to revolve around you. Mum's moving heaven and earth to pay for your school fees next term. And no doubt Dad'll be guilt-tripped into coughing up somehow while my place on the sports tour to South Africa gets cancelled. But as long as you're OK!"

"Maybe it would be better for you, and Dad and Giselle and their brat, if I wasn't here at all."

"Maybe it would. Maybe it'd be easier for everyone."

"What they did, what you did, is not OK," Kat hissed. "I will *never* forgive you for seeing him behind my back."

Charlie shrugged. "And I'll never forgive you for being a first-class bitch. And neither will anyone else."

My head is full of Noah's CSI board as I make my way back along the path. Tomorrow I'll return to the boathouse like he suggested and look more closely at what he's pieced together. I need to know if he's found anything important, even if the others don't care enough. And he's made me wonder what happened to Dom Crawford after last summer.

The moon's up and once my eyes adjust, I don't need to use my phone torch. This is how it would have been for Kat that night. Away from the lights of the house, you soon adapt. We all know this garden so well. We know that the last step down to the lawn is a deeper one, that you duck in the middle as you go through the pergola of roses or get spiked by thorns, that this path down to the beach gets overgrown between our visits. If Kat did take this route that night, she'd have gone along it fast, even in the dark. I was out of the way counting by the horse chestnut tree, the others were busy hiding themselves. And once she was out of the grounds, she could take the path up towards the village. Or go down to the beach and use the water – though none of the paddleboards or kayaks were missing.

Sometimes last summer is so fuzzy, like it happened in a film or I dreamed it all. My mind plays tricks about what happened – if you replay things in your head enough times, that becomes your reality. It's hard to remember, to be sure of what I'm remembering. In my memory, I counted to twenty standing by the tree – but it could have been less or more. The moon was full, the weather clear. Footsteps, laughter. The truth gets blurrier and blurrier.

I sit on the bench with the best view of the house and back in the Wi-Fi zone. Mum has messaged to check I'm OK. They really don't like me being out of their sight. I send back *Fine* then worry that's too lukewarm and they'll phone me – which I stressed was not allowed for the whole of my stay here. I do another message: *Good, thanks.* Then add another: *What happened to Liz's boyfriend Dom from last summer btw? You said she was still seeing him in Bristol.*

While I'm waiting, I check out Dom's website that Noah found. He's good at photography. There are urban shots of street art and industrial buildings in Bristol, but my favourite is the Cornish collection, some of which he must have taken down here last year. There are tin-mine landscapes, deserted beaches and quirky thumbnail shots of lobster pots or colourful fishing nets and buoys.

My phone beeps an alert. Mum has messaged back a cautious *Why do you want to know?*

Jem asked me.

Liz wanted to focus on finding Kat.
I don't think she saw him more than
once afterwards.

OK. Going to sleep now. Night, night.
Love you, Millie. Night, night, Mum xxx

I wasn't really with it last autumn. I wasn't thinking straight. I'd assumed that Dom was still going out with Liz for a while at least. It could have been Dom, not Rob, who Liz was talking about when she said she'd trusted the wrong person. Guilt is a very destructive emotion – that's what Mrs E says. Maybe Liz is in such a state because she blames herself for something. But what does she think happened? I'm confused about it all. Maybe Noah and his incident board are just what I need.

There's a contact email on Dom's website for enquiries on commercial work and I want to type something but don't know what. How do you tactfully ask someone about their relationship with a missing teenager? I try three different drafts before I settle on: *Hey, Dom. This is Millie Thomas. You probably don't remember me but we met at Creek House. I'm Kat Berkley's friend. Can we have a chat about last summer?*

Chatty, friendly, not at all me. I click send.

When I get back inside, the others haven't even twigged I was gone from my room. I pretend I was upstairs reading and lost track of time. Jem's already gone to bed. Matt looks pleased to see me. He's been babysitting Charlie who's worked his way through the beers in the fridge and started on the drinks cabinet. Some of the bottles in there have been knocking around for years. It was a standing joke that Nick would offer the oldies foul cocktails at the New

Year's Eve party, blowing dust off a bottle of something yellow from the last millennium and passing round a jar of bright red cocktail cherries. But no one's laughing tonight as Charlie mixes up spirits and gets louder and louder.

"Millie!" he says, slapping me hard on the back. "Do you wanna see my little brother? Here he is." He sticks his phone too close to my face for me to focus easily. It's a blurry Charlie holding a baby in dungarees. "Jackson's so scute. I mean, cute," he slurs, hugging the screen.

"Definitely cute," I agree.

"Do you know, when he was born, he had these teeny tiny little fingers and fingernails? Amazing. Fancy a Surfer's Colada Sunrise Margarita cocktail?"

"I'm fine, thanks." I retreat to an armchair.

"Go on," he says. "I invented it myself." He sways and the drink sloshes out of the glass leaving a yellow puddle on the rug.

"Go easy, mate," says Matt. "Ancient cream liqueur and that eggnog stuff is not going to be good in the morning."

"Are you fine, Millie? I mean, really?" Charlie sits on the arm of my chair and his eyes try to focus on mine. His breath must be flammable. "'Cos we all know how you felt about Kat. And you were in a bad way last autumn when you…"

"Charlie…" says Matt. "Don't."

My face flushes hot and red.

"Obviously she's my twin and I love her, but she could

be…" He breaks off as he nearly falls from the arm of the chair. "What's the name of those creatures in the Percy Jackson books – the ones who sing and attract you to the rocks?"

"The Sirens?"

He jabs his finger in my direction. "Yessss! Them. She could be a bit like the Sirens."

"I think I'll head off to bed," I say, getting up and squeezing past him. I do not want to get into this conversation. Ever.

"Mills, it's not even eleven thirty. You can't go to bed yet. Can she, Matt? Tell her, Matt." He catches me by the arm. "It's way too early."

Matt sighs. "Maybe an earlier night will do us all good. Then we could go out on the river again tomorrow. Let's have a nice long drink of water, hey?"

Charlie drops his hand, but I don't leave. I look at Matt to see what I should do and tilt my head in Charlie's direction.

"It's all right. I'll look after him," he says to me quietly.

Charlie never used to be like this. Kat joked that his body was his temple. When he got serious about his sport, he began each day with lifting weights and followed a vegan, low sugar diet, faffing about with kale smoothies which clogged up the blender. He always refused any spliffs or cigarettes that anyone offered, and he was never drunk, or aggressive like this afternoon at the pub. Charlie's another casualty of last summer.

Now he's playing music through the large speakers. Loud

dance tracks pulse into the room and he leaps on to the coffee table, vibrating wildly, scattering the fancy magazines and books. "Everybody dance!" he shouts, as Matt reaches up to him, ready to catch him if, *when*, he falls.

Matt's a good friend to him.

But I suppose it's amazing what a guilty conscience can do.

Dear Kat,

I saw your half-brother today. He's cute. Adorable in fact. I only saw a photo. Charlie has it on his phone.

I think you'd have loved little Jackson too if you'd given him half a chance.

Because it's not his fault, is it, who his parents are? And I always liked your dad until we were all meant to hate him. Poor Giselle. If she was expecting to head off into a romantic sunset, she had that dream shattered big time, thanks to you. Did she hate you as much as you hated her?

Millie

Transcript of the police interview between Noah Biscoe and DC Taylor

DC T: For the record this interview is being audio recorded in interview room number 2. The time by the interview clock is 4.30 p.m. and the date is Wednesday 15th August 2018. This interview is being conducted by Detective Constable 3793 David Taylor. Please state your full name clearly for the recording.

NB: *(Clears throat.)* Noah Peter Biscoe.

DC T: And you're resident at 2, Fisherman's Cottages, Powan.

NB: Yes.

DC T: And you're currently 18 years old. What's your date of birth?

NB: It's 2nd July 2000.

DC T: Do you understand why you're here, Noah? You are not under arrest and may terminate this interview now or at any time during its duration.

NB: Not really, no. Not when you could have asked me more questions at home. And I don't understand why you had to haul me off in a police car in front of the whole village either.

DC T: This is a serious matter, Noah. A girl's missing. I'm sure as a concerned citizen you're happy to help with our inquiries. But you're free to leave if you don't want to help us find your girlfriend.

NB: She's not my girlfriend.

DC T: We'll come to that. Let's get through the formalities. You are entitled to free and independent legal advice and I understand that you have declined such advice.

NB: Yes, because I haven't done anything wrong.

DC T: Can you confirm there is no one else present in the room?

NB: Yes. Just you and me, having a great time.

DC T: You do not have to say anything. But it may harm your defence if you do not mention when questioned something which you later rely on in court. Anything you do say may be given in evidence. Do you understand?

NB: Yes.

DC T: I've had the pleasure of meeting your dad in a professional capacity. Still banged up, is he?

NB: I haven't seen him for years. We don't have anything to do with him.

DC T: In for GBH again, is he? I remember when

he assaulted a police officer in St Ives. And he's been done for sexual assault in the past.

NB: Like I said, I don't have anything to do with my dad.

DC T: All right, drop the tone, lad. That winds you up, does it, asking about Mr Biscoe senior?

NB: I am not him. I am nothing like him.

DC T: Very glad to hear it as I'm sure you'll be very cooperative in answering my questions. Let's start with how well you knew Katherine Berkley. How long had you been going out together?

NB: We weren't going out together. We had a thing, briefly.

DC T: A thing? Help me out, Noah, because I'm ancient compared to you and a bit out of date on what's normal these days. Does having a 'thing' mean you slept together? Did you have a sexual relationship with Katherine?

NB: No. It was nothing.

DC T: Beautiful girl like that. Bet you couldn't believe your luck. For the recording, I'm showing Mr Biscoe a photograph of Katherine Berkley.

NB: I know what she looks like.

DC T: I bet you do. In fact, this is a photo we
        retrieved from your bedroom. Along with
        quite a few others of Miss Berkley.

NB: It's not a crime to have photos of a
        friend.

DC T: No, of course not. But it raises questions,
        see, when the particular 'friend' in
        question goes missing. So, I ask you
        again, did you have a sexual relationship
        with her? Don't be embarrassed. Speak up.
        Plenty of lads round here like to sleep
        around with the pick of the visitors given
        half a chance.

NB: No.

DC T: But you wanted one? Like to see yourself
        as a bit of a player? Did Kat refuse to
        sleep with you and that got you angry?

NB: No. It wasn't like that.

DC T: Because I've got to say, pretty, posh girl
        like this, not sure what she'd be seeing in
        you. We all have leagues, don't we? Some
        of us are lucky to meet someone above our
        league and it all works out beautifully
        like that gangly goalkeeper and his missus.
        But I'm looking at Katherine Berkley and
        can't quite believe a girl like that would

be hanging round the son of Aiden Biscoe.

NB: Can I have a drink of water?

DC T: Certainly. Here you go. *(Water poured.)*
        And while you're drinking it, you have
        a think about what you need to tell me.
        (Pause.) When did you first meet Katherine?
        I'm having a quick check with what you
        said to my colleague, PS Harris: "I barely
        knew her". That's what you said.

NB: I meant I didn't know her well. She was
        hard to get to know.

DC T: But you wanted to get to know her. Wanted
        to sleep with her.

NB: Yes… No. I liked her.

DC T: You fancied her? Is that still the word,
        for an old bloke like me?

NB: I suppose, yes.

DC T: So, you fancied her, she showed an
        interest, flirted maybe? Up at Creek House
        or in the village? At the Sea Trout? Where
        was this courtship playing out?

NB: We had an evening at the pub last week -
        Friday - but not just us. Her friend was
        there - the quiet one. Younger. I'm not
        sure of her name.

DC T: Like a chaperone? A third wheel? A big,
        hairy gooseberry? That must have been

157

annoying when you thought you were going on a hot date with Katherine Berkley.

NB: I didn't think it was a date. I saw them earlier in the week when I dropped off some shopping at Creek House and Kat asked me to meet her - them - in the pub. And Kat and I had a good evening and we went for a walk the next day - on the Saturday. We walked along the cliff path.

DC T: That was the 11th, the day before she went missing.

NB: Yes. She was fine and that was the last time I saw her, honest.

DC T: You said you had a 'thing'? Had you met her before this summer?

NB: A bit. When I was a little kid my mum used to take me with her sometimes when she was working there and I'd play in the garden. Maybe she was there then as well as Matt and Jemima de Vries, I don't remember. And then just in passing the last couple of years. Around New Year at the pub, maybe.

DC T: Because she was a frequent visitor to Creek House - every summer holiday and every New Year. And your mum still cleans there, doesn't she? For the recording, Mr Biscoe is nodding. I'm presuming your mum has a set of keys for Creek House. Know where she keeps them, do you?

NB: Well, yes, but…

DC T: You could come and go any time you like to Creek House. Ever go up there when they're not down on their holidays? Ever tempted to pop in and hang out in the big house. Full drinks cabinet, widescreen TV. Get some mates over? Proper job.

NB: Course not.

DC T: So, you've never used your mum's keys to get in there?

NB: Only if there's something that needs doing. We - she makes up the beds, fills the fridge for them before they get here, hoovers. I go and water the patio plants, cut the grass. That kind of thing.

DC T: It's fair to say that you're very familiar with the place, then, Noah? Know the house and gardens better than anyone else round here, it seems to me. All the nooks and crannies. The hiding places. Ever joined in with one of their games of hide-and-seek?

NB: No. Maybe when I was really little. I dunno.

DC T: I'm giving you a pen and a piece of paper,
        Noah. So it's clear in my head and there's
        no misunderstanding, let's see if we can
        get a timetable down for you for the last
        day you saw her - the Saturday - right the
        way through from the moment you leaped out
        of bed in the morning to laying your head
        back on the pillow at bedtime.

NB: I went through all that with the other
        police officer.

DC T: You said you'd headed up country to Exeter
        to see your cousin. I'm a little confused
        about what happened between you saying a
        fond farewell to Katherine on the Saturday
        and Katherine going missing at about 11
        p.m. on Sunday. You don't strike me as the
        sort of lad to be all tucked up in bed
        by that time of night. See, I'm wondering
        if you went along to the party at Creek
        House later on in the evening on Sunday
        to continue your 'thing' with Katherine.

NB: I was in Exeter. I didn't come back till
        the Monday. Mum told me when I got back
        about her going missing. I think Jemima
        had been round.

DC T: Fast driving, empty roads. You could have
        popped back in an hour and a half. Maybe

she led you on, bit of a tease, and you thought it was all going one way and then she called a halt? Is that how it happened?

NB: How what happened? I was up country. Ask my cousin. Can I have another glass of water? *(Water poured.)*

DC T: Did you carry on regardless, Noah? Did it get out of hand and before you knew it, a little too much pressure on her neck maybe and she was dead? All a terrible accident but you were too scared to come forward. For the recording, Mr Biscoe has his head in his hands.

NB: It was nothing like that at all. I never hurt her. I didn't touch her. I would never hurt Kat - or anyone. I helped with the search when I got back. Ask Ali at the pub.

DC T: Of course not, Noah. No one's saying you meant for anything to happen. And don't you worry - we'll be speaking to Ali Ninan and everyone else about you. Won't it be a relief to get it off your chest now, lad? Her poor family are beside themselves. You can help them find some answers.

NB: I want to help her family. Really, I do. But…

DC T: Good lad. Let's have a little break now and I can see if your cousin says you were with him every minute of your time in Exeter. Interview suspended, the time by the interview room clock is 4.43 p.m. *(Recording stopped.)*

"I don't have long," I say, as Noah lets me into the boathouse. This time I've knocked rather than broken in. "I left a note for the others saying I was going to the village shop."

I follow him up the stairs, emerging into the loft space, full of sunshine from the picture window at the far end. It looks so different in the daylight and he's tidied it up. The makeshift bed is pushed to one side and the cups have been washed and stacked. He's tidied himself up too – I can smell his deodorant. Cheap and heavy.

The window's open and the breeze rustles the papers on the table. One on the wall flaps gently. Noah picks up a tin of drawing pins and fixes it down again. In the cold light of day the incident board looks more like a school project than CSI.

"Where shall we start?" he asks.

"I guess I should read everything you've got," I say, like I know what I'm talking about and do this all the time.

He hands me a cardboard box with plastic document wallets and envelopes containing more papers and photos. It's full of pages of lists and data, graphs and scribblings.

I pluck out a couple of sheets. "Did you do all this? It must have taken ages."

"I didn't have much else better to do. These stats and info are all out there, on government websites, and if there's something else you want you can't find, you can make a Freedom of Information request. Do you know how much violent crime happens in Cornwall? How much by a random stranger?"

I shake my head.

"You'll see, from all this, the chances of Kat being taken by a random violent stranger on private rural land at that precise point in time…"

"While I was counting to twenty," I add.

"…are infinitesimal. Like, a million to one."

I flick through the papers and nod as though I understand.

"My theory is either she went of her own free will," he says. He pauses and moistens his lips nervously. "Or, as it's so unlikely to have been a stranger, someone who knew her was responsible for her abduction."

The photographs of the Creekers look out at me from the board. *Someone who knew her, someone who loved her. One of us.*

"And if so, we need a motive." He trails a pencil across our pictures. "I thought that's what you might be able to help me with as a starting point."

I shake my head. "I can't think of a single reason why any of us would want to hurt Kat."

He looks disappointed but what does he expect? Me to trash everyone, myself included? There's no way I'd spill Kat's secrets to him or to anyone. I set down the box. I want to start with the wall. I'd like to reorder it, move things around. I'd like to remove my own picture. But it's not as easy as on TV. Everything is pinned to the wood with a drawing pin or nail or stuck down with thick tape. I'm not going to have that moment when a bit of shuffling around a giant board and standing back in contemplation is going to make it all come clear.

I tell Noah to sit down – his pacing's annoying me and making it hard to concentrate. I start with scraps of police interview transcripts and the newspaper cuttings. I'm familiar with most of the articles. For a while, I cut them out and kept them in my dressing table. Until Mum found them and cleared them away without asking. Back then I read every last word looking for some clue about what had happened to Kat. But they had little of any use to say. They didn't know who Kat was, not like I did. There were pieces on social media, exam pressure and holidays from hell. One on the effect of incomers like Nick and Anna on property prices in Cornwall, and several articles about the number of people who go missing.

"Do you think she's dead?" he asks suddenly. He blinks at me, like he's asked a normal question.

"I don't like to think about that," I say. And definitely don't like to talk about it.

"Seems to me that killing someone isn't the tricky bit. It's easy to murder someone – an argument that gets out of hand, a push that leads to a bad knock on the head."

Please stop. Nothing like that is easy.

"I mean, circumstances sometimes, bad things can happen. Right?" He rubs at his forehead. "This isn't coming out well."

"I can see why your babysitting jobs dried up," I say.

"My point is that although it's terrible, it's easy to kill someone. I see how it can happen. But disposing of the body afterwards – that's the tricky part."

I shiver, even though the sun's streaming in. These are the exact things I've been trying not to think about all year. I've shoved those fears in a box in my head and rammed it shut. It's been my only way of coping.

He picks up a pen and clicks it on and off. "You'd need strength, nerve, knowledge, planning, resources. And a heap of luck that it all goes to plan. Killing someone in the first place, especially if by accident, is not the same thing at all. Even using the sea, it's difficult to manhandle a body, unseen, and tip it off somewhere the tides won't bring it back again. You'd have to weigh it down."

"Don't. It's too horrible to think of that happening to Kat."

"I'm not saying that did happen to her," he says. "It'd be much easier with a boat to go further out to sea. Obviously. But that requires more planning, local knowledge of the tides."

My eyes flicker towards the stairs. His rowing boat's tied up down below. He's the one with the very small boat *and* the knowledge.

"My little boat barely fits one person, let alone a dead body as well," he says, following my gaze. "You're gonna need a bigger boat. *Jaws* – the movie. Famous line." He gets up and points to the tiny font of the Tide Tables pinned up, with the evening of the party circled. "And low tide on the river by Creek House that night means you can't navigate it."

I sit on the camp bed and hug my knees to my chest, looking up at the pictures of Kat on the wall. Kat from a year ago, frozen in time. She looks out at me again from one of the pictures in her bikini and hat. Maybe Noah and all his paperwork can help me find some answers as to how she disappeared into thin air. Because someone knows something. I lick my dry lips and ask the question I've been working up to. "Let's go with the idea that Kat could have chosen to go – and that's way more likely than running into a psychopath in the woods that night. So, what if she wanted to get away, without a trail of tickets and passport checks? What if Kat herself wanted a lift on a small boat to make it harder to find her?"

"You mean, who could she pay to take her somewhere, no questions asked?"

"Yes. And where could she get to, practically?" I stand up to look at the map on the wall.

He moves beside me, his arm brushing mine as he traces a line across the sea. "Assuming we're not talking world cruise on a liner, next stop out of Cornwall is Brittany on the French coast."

My finger follows his across the map.

"Kat loved her French exchange, didn't stop talking about it."

France is a big country. I reckon she could manage not to be found. I like to think that. I like to think she could have gone there. In my head, she's in a floaty dress in a field of sunflowers, like an impressionist painting. Slightly smudged, slightly blurred, hard to make her out. Indistinct. But glowing. Sometimes she's sipping an espresso at a pavement café in Paris, her face shaded by a wide-brimmed hat.

I try to shake off the images as Noah's asking me questions, but I can't focus on his voice. I get these periods when I think about Kat and the rest of the world seems to shut down around me.

I don't think I'll ever get my head all to myself again.

"Millie? Did the police look into that?" Noah's agitated, pulling on my arm. "Millie!"

"Did the police look into what?" I blink to shake away Kat and the sunflowers.

"Whether she went to France, back to where she'd been?"

"Her mum asked the family she stayed with on the exchange trip and they said they hadn't heard anything from her. The police followed it up too with the ferry companies and the French authorities. Her passport was missing but it's never been used."

"But if her plan was to travel secretly by private boat she wouldn't show up on any French records," Noah says. "And there'd be no trace of her here. No dead body. It makes sense."

I wish he'd stop mentioning her dead body. "Kat was, *is*, too clever to leave traces if she doesn't want to. It'd have to be someone who was up for dropping a sixteen-year-old off in another country without proper immigration checks, and who's kept their mouth firmly shut ever since."

Noah rummages quickly through his notes in the box looking for something. "Here: I did a list of everyone I know with a registered boat kept at Powan marina. And made a note of who was around on the twelfth, not off on a fishing trip. But they were all accounted for – none of them could have been creeping through the woods at your place."

"You were looking for someone snatching her and getting rid of a body that night," I say. "If they were giving her a lift, it could have been any of the following days, couldn't it? All she needed to do was lie low until the boat was lined up and ready to go. We need to look again."

He spreads out the sheets on the floor and we crouch down, scanning columns. "Most of these are rock-solid guys. But I suppose maybe this one – Chris. He sells things from time to time that you know have fallen off the back of a boat, shifts stuff around the coast that he shouldn't. Recreational drugs – nothing really bad. He might have been up for a cash-in-hand trip. Ask no questions. And the dates fit for when his boat was in harbour."

"Should we go and see him? You know him, right?"

"Chris isn't the kind of guy I normally hang out with, or want to cross-examine."

Kat didn't have all of Noah's local knowledge, didn't have info literally stuck round the room like us. But she did have a knack for getting what she wanted. "You think Kat would have been able to link up with him?"

"Powan's a pretty small place. Wouldn't have been that hard if you asked the right people."

"We have to speak to him today," I say.

I'm no body-language expert but even I can tell Noah's not keen. He chews at his thumbnail. "I don't want to owe blokes like that a favour."

I point at his stupid CSI board. "What's all this for otherwise? I'm leaving tomorrow."

"All right. Let's see if he's around. But if he's off fishing, he could be away for a week."

"And what about the rest of this? These?" I pick up an envelope of photos. "Can I take them to look through?"

He hesitates. "I suppose. If I get them back after."

I put the photos in my pocket. My hands are shaking. It's one thing emailing Dom, or me and Noah coming up with theories. But now we're going to talk to some dodgy man. *Interview* him to see if Kat got on his boat.

It's opening up Schrödinger's box like Matt talked about and seeing what really happened to Kat.

I'm not sure I'm ready to know.

Dear Kat,

I think I get what Matt meant now.

If we don't open the box, you can exist in two states.

Dead or alive.

Is it best to let it lie? I think you told me that once.

Lots of love,

M xxx

9 August 2018

August 2018 wasn't panning out the way I'd looked forward to for months. I'd got my wish to stay around Creek House rather than the surf trip Matt suggested, but it hadn't been fun. The last couple of days had been a write-off.

Kat was still mad at her dad which meant she was mad at all of us. She and Jem had had some sort of falling-out after breakfast which hadn't blown over yet. Charlie and Matt were spending all their time playing sport or away from the house. Liz was slagging off Rob and Giselle and draping herself over Dom at every opportunity. He seemed both amused and horrified by the whole situation and was taking increasingly long walks with his camera. Mum and Anna were being supportive. Nick had retreated to his work phone.

Dad texted me from home to ask if I was having fun and remind me to do some GCSE maths if I was bored. I'd replied that I'd made cookies, everything was brilliant, and I was revising probability. Which was sort of true: I was working out the probability of the party going ahead on Sunday night and had settled on 10%. I'd been looking forward to playing hide-and-seek and board games but now needed a flow chart and a series of Venn diagrams to work out who was talking to who exactly.

I'd hoped we could all get together this evening and start planning the party, but the Creekers were going separate ways. Charlie had gone out without saying where to, which probably meant he was seeing his dad and Giselle at their hotel. Matt and Jem went out for a meal with their parents at a gastro pub somewhere – possibly discussing as a family whether they should rethink having all the rest of us to stay in their idyllic holiday home twice a year.

I thought I should stay at the house in case Kat needed me, but she made it clear she was going to bed early with period pain and was not to be disturbed. I was banished from my own room with a choice of TV on my own or hanging with Mum and Liz. Dom and his camera were having another evening out. I chose to take a bottle of wine from the fridge and sit in the woods. On my own. A party for one.

I wanted to dull the feelings, at least for tonight. To feel older, like the others. Less of a misfit. I unscrewed the bottle and tried the wine. It made me shudder. How did people like drinking this stuff?

All the other Creekers were growing up away from me. I'd always been the youngest, but now they were interested in completely different things. I was the little kid in the corner that they were obligated to play the occasional board game with to keep me quiet, before they went back to snogging each other or having a spliff or an existential crisis.

The wood pigeons were cooing in the branches above me, and the breeze was blowing from the creek so I could hear the rhythmic strike of oars into the water from a passing rowing gig. Maybe it was Noah. Why Kat had suggested he came to the pub on Friday, I didn't know. Except that she'd asked him right in front of Matt who'd immediately left the room. Noah had only popped by with a bag of food his mum had asked him to bring. He was thin and gangly, like a weasel, and he never looked you in the eye; not Kat's usual confident type at all. She normally talked about boys from school called Tristram or Bertie who had their own car. She'd gone on about someone called Xavier on her French exchange. I shuddered at what I'd seen between her and Matt. And then there was the gift of the bikini and slimy Dom. It was all very hurtful and hard to keep up with. I'd had hardly any time on my own with Kat and now I had to share her with Noah too.

I drank some more, faster this time, so that I didn't taste it so much. It dribbled down my chin. I wanted all the confusing thoughts in my head to go away. I leaned back against the tree trunk, as it was easier than standing. That was too difficult because the trees were swaying. I gradually eased my way down until my bottom was on the ground. This wasn't the fun I'd thought it'd be. In fact, it was making things worse, not better. Now I was more miserable, sick and dizzy. And I shouldn't have taken the bottle without asking. Great, a dose of guilt was adding to my problems.

A twig snapped behind me and Kat walked into the clearing, looking flushed. "Mills! I practically tripped over you. What are you doing here?" She put her hands on her hips. "Well, well, well. Millie-Moo getting off her head in the bushes."

"Where have you been?" My lips were numb, like they didn't belong to me, but I managed to wrangle them into word shapes and form sentences. Though they didn't sound quite right in my head. "You said you were going to lie down. You said you had period pain."

"Because no male ever questions that, Mills. It makes them leave you alone. The ones you don't want to see."

"You don't have to lie to me, though," I said. "We tell each other *everything*. Where you been. Where you've been?" The letter V was difficult to say with my new lips.

I wished she'd sit down so I didn't have to crane my neck. I stared instead at her feet on the ground in front of me. She wore flip-flops and sand from the creek beach was on her toes, clinging to the damp.

I looked up at her, my head heavy and wobbly on my neck. She was blurry and moving from side to side. Were there two of her? Had she been for a paddle? "Truth, Kat," I forced out. "Tell the truth."

"Why is everyone obsessed with the truth? Let sleeping dogs lie. That's best. *The truth is rarely pure and never simple:* Oscar Wilde. Did you know that, Mills? If in doubt in a quiz, say Oscar Wilde. He has all the best quotations."

She jumped up on a log and clutched her hand to her breast. "*We are all in the gutter but some of us are looking at the stars.*"

My head was hurting. I couldn't keep up and somehow we were talking about Oscar Wilde. I looked at the sky, but it wasn't dark yet and no stars were visible. Just treetops and glimpses of cloud. The effort made me dizzier and more nauseous.

Kat crouched beside me. "People to see, places to go. There are some things it's best not to know, Mills."

A glob of mascara was stuck on the end of her lashes and I wanted to wipe it away. "The truth, Kat. It's always best to know the truth."

She smiled and her eyes narrowed. "Is it? Even the truth about lies? Shall we play true or false? You like playing games, Millie. And you're nearly as good at them as me."

It was a compliment but felt like an insult. Or was it the other way round? It was sometimes hard to tell with Kat.

"All our families excel at it – bluffing, cheating, knowing when to take a risk and when to fold," she said. "Full of secrets and lies. Never the truth."

"I don't know what you mean. What secrets and lies? Is this about Giselle again?"

"Every family is full of them, Mills. If you think yours is any different, you're wrong."

"Mine's not like that. It's yours that's the disaster zone."

She frowns. "You always tell Mumsie and Daddy exactly what you're doing – true or false?"

"True."

"Do they know you're here now, Millie? Getting sloshed

176

on a fancy bottle of wine? Good job I'm here to look after you. I think you've had quite enough." She took the bottle from me and poured the remaining dribble of liquid on to the ground. "And do you think they tell you everything? Did your dad tell you why he was arguing with my mum on New Year's Day? Begging her to be reasonable?"

"What do you mean? What's my dad got to do with anything?"

"Ask him. Ask him why he and my mum were having an argument after lunch. And why they were together down in the village when your dad had made a big thing of driving off for a meeting. Ask him why he hasn't come down this summer."

"He had to work."

"Really? At the weekend too? Think about it, Mills. Maybe you should ask your mum. Are they arguing a lot? Distant with each other? True or false?"

If I could only clear my head of all this fuzziness, I'd be able to understand. "You're trying to confuse me because I asked where you'd been. Who have *you* been seeing?"

That was the important thing. She was throwing nonsense around to distract me from that. Bluffing. I tried to stand but my legs didn't want to take my weight.

She placed her finger on her lips and shushed me. "It's all getting too complicated. I've had enough of all the lies. It should be simple."

Kat turned and disappeared back into the trees. I wasn't

sure if I'd even seen her. She was like a sprite, a tree spirit, who'd been and gone in an instant. And cast a vicious spell.

Dear Kat,

Some people are wreckers. They can't bear it when others have something they don't. They'd rather smash it, scratch it. Ruin it. Destroy it forever rather than let their friend have it.

Can you imagine that? Can you? And when I say 'some people', Katherine, I'm talking about you.

Love,

M xx

My experience of actual fishermen is basically zero. I'm expecting a guy with a beard in a chunky jumper sitting at the harbour mending nets, singing sea shanties.

Chris's house is one of the modern terraced ones on the edge of the village. There's an old trailer taking up the front garden. As we walk up the path, Noah gestures to the lounge window. A man in a tracksuit is watching Peppa Pig on a massive TV, with a toddler dressed up as a princess bouncing on his lap.

"Maybe we should come back when he isn't so busy," Noah says.

But I ring the doorbell.

Chris doesn't roll out the red carpet for visitors, standing on his doorstep with a can of Red Bull in one hand and scratching at his groin with the other. His hair's tied back in a ponytail and he has the sort of wispy moustache that was popular in the Seventies. Noah does the greetings. By which I mean he mutters "All right, Chris. This is Millie." And then pokes me in the ribs to say something.

"I'm hoping you'll be able to help us," I stutter.

"I doubt it," he says. The kid pulls at his leg. Peppa Pig is blaring at full volume.

"It's about my friend, Kat Berkley. The girl who went missing last year."

His eyes narrow. "Why would I know anything about that?"

"I wondered if she'd ever asked you for a ride on your boat?"

A ride? Why did I say that? I've made it sound like a fairground ride. "A trip, I mean."

He shakes his head. The kid starts crying. "Go back and watch it," he tells her. "Daddy'll be there in a minute."

"A trip to France," I say.

As soon as I say France, his expression changes. He starts closing the door.

I block it with my hand. "Look, we don't want to cause you any trouble. We're not going to tell the police anything, are we, Noah?"

I look across at Noah. This is news to him because I guess he might want to speak to the police, to clear his name. Not that they've listened to him so far.

"We know how to keep quiet, don't we?" I nudge him.

"Yeah, you know my dad. Seems like you owe him a favour after that thing that went down in Penzance. And you know I'd never grass anyone up."

"Yes, and er, snitches get stitches," I say.

Chris laughs – a huge, belly laugh. "You crack me up, you do. Snitches get stitches! I'll give you a couple of minutes, that's all. As a favour to this one's dad."

We sit on the edge of the settee. It's sticky. His daughter's eating jam on toast in between sucking her thumb and wiping it along the edge of the seats. Peppa Pig and George are jumping noisily in muddy puddles.

"Did Kat ask you about taking her to France?" I show Chris one of the pictures of her I took from the boathouse. But he barely glances at it. He knows exactly who I'm talking about.

Chris pulls at his earlobe. "If she had asked me, I'd have had to say no – seeing as dropping people in France without proper customs and border checks, that's not allowed."

As I'm trying to work my way through all the negatives in what he says, he winks.

"If Katherine *had* asked you, how much, roughly, *wouldn't* you have charged her?"

"Roughly £2,000 per person. That's what I *wouldn't* have asked for, you get me?"

Noah lets out a low whistle. "That's way more than the ferry out of Plymouth."

So much money. Hard-earned money given to someone like Chris.

"That'd be a bargain, mate. I've got a proper fishing vessel with an experienced skipper (me), safety features, navigation. I want to make sure I come back to this little one after every *fishing* trip." He tickles his daughter and she giggles, spraying toast crumbs from her mouth. "You should hear how much the people smugglers out of France are charging – and that's for a heap-of-shit inflatable dinghy. Scum. Anyway, like I said, I would have told your friend. I am *not* doing that sort of thing."

"Course not," says Noah.

"And I wouldn't have said she could tag along on my next fishing trip. Though that ended up not being till the next weekend."

My head's whirring, with what he did or didn't do. And how to ask questions in a way that will get a straight answer.

He slaps his hands on his thighs and stands. "Time's up. Smells like I need to change a nappy." He towers above both of us on the sticky settee.

Noah and I head to the door.

"Don't be coming over again," he says. Although Chris is smiling, he manages to make it seem like a threat. "Give my best to your dad, Noah. Tell him to drop by dreckly when he's out."

Out from where? This guy talks in riddles all the time.

The princess toddler hands me her tiara and I kneel to put it back on her head. I'm rubbish with small kids. I normally make them cry. This one grins at me. "You're a perfect princess," I say. "Pink's my favourite colour too."

Chris beams and ruffles her hair. "She's cracking, isn't she?"

The girl continues beaming up at me like I'm her new best mate.

"I'm sorry you haven't found your friend," Chris says, in a softer tone. "I didn't say nothing to the police – because she never turned up. And I won't be saying nothing to them or

182

to you two about this again, understood?"

Noah nods and they shake hands. Chris holds his grip until his knuckles whiten, and Noah flinches. "You owe me one now, my handsome. And I know whose fault it is if the police come knocking, don't I?" He drops his hold and Noah flexes out his fingers before heading straight down the path, calling for me to come on.

I hesitate, torn between asking more and retreating like Noah.

"She was a real stunner, your friend," says Chris. "I hung around for an hour in case they came but then I had to take the boat out. Tides." The door slams shut.

I wait until Noah and I are well away from Chris's house and sitting on the wall together outside the village shop before I say anything at all. "Do you think Chris took Kat to France?"

"He says he didn't." Noah's still nursing his hand.

"But £2000 is a lot of money – worth keeping his mouth shut for."

Noah chews at his thumbnail. "If he says he didn't, that's the end of it. Whatever. Even if he bumped her on the head and tipped her overboard. End of." He stops when he sees the look on my face. "I'm not saying he did that. He's not the most reliable but I do believe him that he didn't take her."

Images of Kat drifting round France fill my head again. It's reassuring to know that she was actively looking into it and my hunch was right. That I can get inside her head when I want to.

"You realize there's absolutely nothing from today I can share with the police," says Noah. "Don't think that because he's all cuddly with his daughter that he wouldn't think twice about breaking my legs. Or worse."

Unlike Noah, I don't want to share anything with the police. I just want to know myself that Kat had a way to get to France.

The church bells strike. "I've got to get back," I say. "I've been gone ages. I said I was going to the shop."

"You're getting good at this," he says. "Covering your tracks. And you handled Chris well." He gets to his feet. "We make a good team, don't we? It's a shame you're leaving so soon. If we keep working at it, something will come of it, I'm sure."

I smile at my new friend. "You're right. I'll call you later when I can." I watch as he walks back towards his house, hands in pockets, head down. I go into the shop and browse the shelves of biscuits and chocolate bars for something to buy the others. But I'm not really seeing anything. I'm thinking back over what Chris said. He gave Kat a price *per person* and he said he waited an hour in case *they* came. Not *she*. Not in case *she* came.

Who was she planning to take with her on the boat?

I close my eyes and take a deep breath. Could it even have been me?

184

10 August 2018

When I woke up, I thought Kat must have gone for a run already. Her bed was unmade. Normally she'd wake me up, stumbling around for her kit, flushing the loo with its ancient plumbing that rattled through the walls. But today my head was throbbing enough on its own. I was dying. Kat had left the curtains closed but the light that sneaked through the flimsy cotton and round the edges was way too bright. I groaned and pulled the duvet up over my head. But the smell of my own breath was too much. It was rank.

I didn't want to move because that would make me puke. But I had to get out of bed because otherwise I'd throw up all over the duvet. I didn't make it as far as the bathroom, or even the door. I threw up into the wastepaper basket – which was so gross that I threw up all over again. It was made of wicker, and if I'd thought I was going to live to see another day, I'd have been worried about owning up to Anna that I'd ruined it. I groaned and clutched my stomach.

I couldn't remember getting into bed. I was still wearing my normal clothes and one sock. My nightshirt was on the back of the chair where I'd left it yesterday morning. I'd had a strange dream about Kat in the forest being Titania in *A Midsummer Night's Dream*.

My phone was buzzing. Really loudly. It stopped but then started up again. I crawled back towards the bed and reached up on to the bedside table, groping for the phone with my eyes still half shut against the bright light. It was Dad. Of course it was. Who else had a sixth sense that something could be keeping me from studying on my holiday? If I didn't answer, he might call Mum and she'd come up to the landing and smell the vomit. I pressed the button and summoned my voice from somewhere very deep inside. "Dad?"

"Morning, Mills. Just checking in."

All these calls. He should just have come on the holiday and spoken to me in real life. It was the first time I could remember that he hadn't come. He couldn't get the time off work, but he wasn't too busy to inflict all these checks on me. "About to go out on the paddleboards," I said. "So much fun. I'll call you later. Bad signal. Weather…" I pressed the red button to end the call and laid my head back down on the carpet. I vaguely remembered that I'd meant to ask him about something, but it was all too fuzzy now. Something Kat had said. I needed to sleep.

*

Kat had managed to get me off the carpet and into the bathroom. She propped me up against the edge of the bath.

"Have a shower, Mills. You'll feel better. Trust me on this one."

I nodded – the smallest of motions so as not to bring on more nausea. "Don't tell Mum. Or Dad."

She laid her hand on her heart. "Of course not. You and I keep each other's secrets, don't we?" She handed me a towel. "You can use my shampoo if you like. I've opened the bedroom windows to get rid of the smell." Her nose wrinkled slightly. "And I love you very much, Mills, but I'm not picking lumps of sick out of a wastepaper basket for anyone. I'll put it in the wheely bin and blame Matt and Charlie if anyone says anything."

"Thank you," I said.

"Throwing up in a bin is the sort of gross thing either of them would do."

"Thank you," I said again. I needed my brain to function better to have a proper conversation. There were more words in there, somewhere.

"I'll bring up a flat Diet Coke and a rice cake to nibble. Guaranteed to settle your stomach. Maybe skip whole bottles of wine in the future. Binge drinking is very overrated."

She got to the door and paused. "Do try and get better in time for tonight, Mills. Don't forget you're coming with me for a drink with Noah."

Even the word 'drink' made my stomach flip. And I still didn't see why we had to go anywhere with Noah. We never had before. I managed a strangled "Why?".

"Because I'm asking you to. I never ask you for anything so I'm sure you can do this tiny thing for me."

"Ask Jem instead," I groaned.

She sighed. "Jem and I… Well, I'd rather take you, Millie Moo." She smiled at me and I nodded my head slightly, very carefully so I didn't puke again. It was nice that she wanted *me* to go.

"I'm going to get the stuff to settle your stomach. But Millie, liven up. I don't want you to be a wet dishcloth all evening with Noah. Oh, and if you could happen to drop our plans into conversation with the others, that'd be good too."

I peeled off my clothes and stood in the shower, letting the water wash over me. Right now, I couldn't even make it downstairs. I didn't want to go and sit in a pub, especially with a man-boy who stared unblinkingly at you when he spoke. I didn't have a clue what I'd talk to him about. I'd rather spend the remaining days of the holiday with Kat, on our own.

I breathed in the smell of the shampoo and washed my hair. Kat was right – I was starting to feel more human. A day of calmly sitting around the garden, listening to audiobooks, seemed achievable. Kat was patching me up. That's what best friends do.

I honestly didn't know what I would do without her.

The others had only just got up when I returned from the village, my head still buzzing from our talk with Chris. They were grateful for the cheap biscuits and fresh bread from the shop. I've got a few minutes in our room before we go on a walk Kat used to love – Charlie's suggestion.

The rest of us exchanged looks. It's the kind of thing we're here to do – to remember Kat. But it has the definite added bonus of being a good way to keep Charlie out of trouble. He can't get into a fight on a footpath and they don't serve beer at the National Trust kiosk halfway round.

I lift the edge of my mattress and peep at the big envelope from the chest of drawers again. It's no use pretending I haven't found it, that I don't know what's inside. But who hid it here? Whose secret have I found? It's not mine and not the little cousins'. The de Vries family have a whole massive house here and another in London where they can hide anything. Why would any of them pick the chest of drawers in our room? I don't want to draw the obvious conclusion, but I have to. I'm only left with one possible person: Kat.

I drop the mattress back into place and spread out the photos I brought from the boathouse on the duvet. I focus on the selfies of Noah and Kat. I don't recognize the background and I can't tell when they were taken. They were snapped one after the other like a stop-animation spread. The kind of pics lovers take in a montage in the movies. Lovers, not friends. Not barely-know-each-other friends. They're both smiling in all of them, and one of Noah's arms is extended holding the phone, the other round Kat's shoulders. In the first one she's got her arm round his waist, beaming, and then both arms wrapped around him and then her kissing him on the cheek. Why would she do that? In the last one there's a look on Noah's face that might be surprise. I don't know him well enough to tell. Kat looks … well, like the cat that got the cream.

None of it makes sense. That evening the three of us went out to the pub, she flirted, for sure, but she wasn't all over him like a rash. Only the odd tap on the knee as she leaned in to ask another question about Noah's boring routines and what his mum did. Lots of hair-flicking and her tinkly laugh. He was wearing a new shirt – one that still had the folds from the packaging and a slight chemical smell. I was sipping my non-alcoholic drinks and trying not to be overwhelmed by the combined smell of beer and cheesy chips. I don't think Noah wanted me to be there. *I* didn't want me to be there.

I check my email. Still no reply from Dom. I pull up his website again and look harder for a contact number which I eventually find in an old reply to a comment. I call it before I chicken out. No answer. The recorded message is the standard one for the network. I leave my number and a message: "*Er, hi. This is Millie, Kat Berkley's friend. Can you call me back as soon as possible, please? Thanks. Bye.*" I sound about twelve.

I'm half relieved he didn't answer. What do I even say to him? *I was wondering if you were sleeping with a sixteen-year-old last summer? Or if you were creeping round the garden that night Kat disappeared? Oh, and did you plan to run off to France together? Thanks so much.* I'll think about what to say later.

I pick up the photos scattered on the bed and stack them inside my notebook. "Where even *is* this?" I whisper, peering at the building barely visible in the background of one of the selfies. A cottage with white gables and a green door which I don't recognize at all. I call Noah and, unlike Dom who has an actual life somewhere, he picks up within two rings.

"The photos of you and Kat that were in that set I brought back, when were they taken?" I ask him. I don't have time for any small talk and we're both bad at it.

"You mean the ones outside? It was the morning after the pub. Early. I opened the door and there she was, friendly as anything, saying she wanted to take me up on the offer of a walk."

I try to think back to that morning. Kat was out when I got up, and I got roped into a morning of shopping with Mum and Anna. She didn't tell me where she'd been.

"I had some work to do. But she came with me," he adds.

"What work? What's the house in the background?" I'm speaking quickly, back on Kat's trail again. Finding out things she'd kept from me.

"It's one of the other holiday homes my mum looks after: Friar's Cottage. It's about a mile on from the village. Kat came with me when I dropped off a new kettle. The last people had managed to break it, and block the septic tank."

"Was Friar's Cottage still empty when Kat went missing?"

"I think there was a week's gap before the next people came. So, yes, it was empty."

"Would the police have searched it?"

"Why would they? I suppose they could have knocked on the door like they did with other houses in the village. But it's further away."

"But if no one answered, if they looked through the windows and saw nothing and nobody but an empty rental…" My mind's whizzing ahead, imagining all the scenarios. "Did you go inside it with Kat?"

"She came in, yes. I used the set of keys at the cottage. They're kept in a key safe by the front door. Like you have at Creek House."

"Did Kat see you press in the number?"

"I *told* her the number – she got the keys out while I was checking round the garden. We went in, we swapped the kettles over, we left. That was it. Then she had to get back. I didn't see her again. She didn't even reply to my messages later."

I'm starting to see Noah's attraction to Kat and the reason for the evening at the pub and those stupid moments in the photos. And why she didn't need to contact him again.

"From Creek House, how long to walk there?"

"Probably an hour. Head along the creek, hit the village and then cut up along the footpath to the route across the cliffs. Do you think she waited there until she could get on a boat?"

"It's a possibility. Can I have a look?" I have to see it for myself, follow the trail Kat's left for me.

"But it's probably got holidaymakers in there," says Noah.

"We'll work something out. I should be able to meet you at your house at about three. Have your mum's set of keys ready so we can get inside Friar's Cottage."

I knew I had nothing to be jealous of with Noah. My finger traces the edge of Kat's face in the last photo. Kat dropped him once she'd got what she wanted.

Dear Kat,

Maybe this is progress. I don't need to share all my thoughts with you at every hour of the day.

I have a new friend. One who doesn't tell me what to do.

From,

M xxx

"Hello?" I repeated into the phone, barely daring to hope. I looked around to check there was no sign of Mum and Dad back at the house or of the other Creekers still down on the beach. "Kat, is that you?" I whispered.

Her familiar voice answered with: "Are you alone, Mills?"

I steadied myself against a tree. Kat was alive. She wasn't a bloated body lying on a slab at the morgue, or dead in a ditch somewhere. She was OK.

And therefore so was I.

Kat had chosen to call me. Not Jem, not lover-boy Matt, not her twin: *me*. I whispered a hundred questions. Was she hurt? Had somebody taken her? Where was she now? Etc, etc. I could have cut it short with a simple: "What the hell, Kat?"

She didn't answer any of my questions anyway, except to say she was fine. She had plenty of questions of her own. Was her dad there? Was Giselle with him? Had he cried? Was her mum still throwing herself at Dom? Was Jem crying? What about Matt? Charlie? The questions went on.

None of them were about me.

"Your parents have literally just been to see an actual dead body in case you'd drowned at sea. They're scared you're dead, Kat. Or worse, chained up in a basement somewhere by a pervert. And what about Charlie? He's losing it. What about me? It's been so horrible, I can't…"

"Sorry if you're upset, Millie, but I need you to listen to me. I need a little time to work out exactly what I want to do. We…" My signal was breaking up. I stopped pacing and held the phone up high and then back to my ear.

"We what? I lost you then. What should we do?"

"Is there going to be a press conference?"

"No one's said anything about that," I said. "They think no one else is involved and you're not a danger to yourself. At this stage, you're just another teenager who's run away for a bit. A Low Risk Misper if you want the lingo. It's quite common actually."

She was quiet. Maybe because I'd basically told her she was nothing special and wasn't going to make the *News at Ten*. And maybe because the police had called it right. She was just another teenager who'd run away for a bit. A drama queen. "You might be in the local paper," I added. "It's called the *Cornish Herald*, I think."

I listened for any background noise to tell me where she was. I thought I could hear the whirr of an appliance – a washing machine on spin? Either she was in a launderette or she was in a house doing her washing. Very rock and roll.

"When are you coming back, Kat?" Why was she putting us all through this? Sounded like there was no great master plan, no noble journey. All the terrible upset, the searching … was it just a plan to make everyone feel bad? Was that what this was about? Was she waiting for some response from her parents that would tick a box for her that meant she could come back? Maybe she wanted her dad to leave Giselle and get back with her mum – but that was never going to happen.

The sick sensation that had lived in my stomach since the game of hide-and-seek was being replaced with fury. Kat was a selfish cow for doing this. The only thing hurting Kat was that she was the star of this show but couldn't watch it in person.

"Come back, Kat. Please. You could say you banged your head and got amnesia and now you remember who you are. I won't say anything."

"Don't be ridiculous, Mills."

I wasn't being ridiculous. She was the one who seemed to have staged her own disappearance for attention. *I* was trying to help.

"I need you to do something for me," said Kat. "And you have to promise to say nothing. I mean, *nothing* to anybody."

"I promise, cross my heart. But you *are* coming back eventually?" I couldn't bear the alternative.

"It's complicated," she said. Like she was the adult, shutting me up with a 'We'll see'. Carrying on with her dumb plan wasn't going to make it any less complicated; any idiot could work that out.

"Will you go to that beach – the one we talked about in Greece?"

"What? What beach? No. Listen to me, Millie, I need you to bring me something. I've left a bag I need in the old fridge in the cellar. You know the one. I couldn't get back in to pick it up that night. Nick was on the phone in the hall. Please, Mills."

While she told me what she wanted and how I wasn't to look in the bag, I was processing what she'd said about Greece. She'd dismissed it, barely knew what I was talking about. All that talk about going round the Greek islands after my A-levels, that must have all been *me*, me planning and her nodding and humouring me, not even listening properly. A fantasy.

"And I need some more money," she added. "Plans have changed a bit and it's not enough."

I wanted to pin her against a wall and scream at her. I wanted to know what plans and why they'd changed and why she couldn't change them again and come home. "Where do I get money from?"

"You're naturally devious, I'm sure you'll think of something," she said. She sounded annoyed and impatient, tutting as though *I* was the unreasonable one. "How much have you got in your bank account?"

Everything I'd been saving from birthday and Christmas money to do a trip with Kat. Emphasis on the '*with*'. Not scrimped and saved to stump up for her to go and leave me behind.

Kat needed my help. She needed me to get the bag and

197

to get her more money. She didn't care how I'd suffered these last few days. She was treating me much as she always did. It didn't occur to her that I wouldn't keep quiet and do exactly what she asked.

But *she* needed *me*. It was *me* who had the power for once.

I could do exactly what she asked me to do.

Or not.

"I can't leave the grounds on my own," I said. "Dad's here now and he thinks I'm going to be snatched by the same mystery lunatic who abducted you. Come at five while most of them are out and wait for me in the summerhouse. I'll get you the bag and some money, and I'll make sure there's no one else around."

"But…" she began.

"It has to be there or nowhere," I said, starting to shake a little. "No one goes in there any more and you can't see it from the house."

I ended the call. *I* cut *her* off. We were doing things on my terms this time.

Dear Kat,
 "Sorry if you're upset, Millie."
 That's what you said.
 Sorry. Not sorry.
 Not a proper sorry.
 A victim-blaming sorry.

Implying that I'm the one who should be sorry for my defective feelings, for being over-sensitive, stupid or unreasonable. Take your pick.

But YOU should have been sorry, Kat.

This was all on YOU, not me.

YOU.

M xxx

The walk with the others was good. If I'm honest, it was better for Kat not being on it. Now I come to think about it, she usually moaned or got a blister. But I didn't mention that to Charlie. He was more like his old self – admiring the view, patting a horse, doing pine-cone ambushes. It was a long walk – six miles. Which is why they're surprised when we get back and I ask if I can borrow a bike as part of my new fitness regime. "Life's short," I say. "You have to make the most of what you've got."

I puff up the hill to Noah's house on a bike that's too big for me and then cycle with him to Friar's Cottage, arriving red and sweaty. The cottage is as it looked in the picture. The green door tastefully standing out against the white paintwork. It has a cutesy front garden set up to please holidaymakers with decorative bright-painted wooden buoys and a lobster pot which has never been near the sea. All very Instagrammable.

"We shouldn't go in when it's rented out," says Noah. "We should wait till changeover day."

"You can wait till next Friday or Saturday, Noah, but I'm leaving tomorrow morning. You wanted my help. Don't wimp out on me."

"If she *was* here…" He pinches the bridge of his nose. "I mean, here, of all places. It looks bad for me. It's a link to me."

"Let's find out first before we worry about it."

He stares down at his feet.

I look at my watch. "Do you know how hard it was to get up here today without the others knowing?" I say. "We're doing it. We knock and if the holidaymakers are in, we say you wanted to check the tank thingy."

"The septic tank. In the garden."

"Or the kettle, then. If I were on holiday, I'd be pleased that you were looking at it."

"And if they're not in?"

"We go in anyway and they'll never know."

"Mum could get into trouble for this. What are we looking for?"

"No one's going to get into trouble. I want to see if it's possible Kat used it, stayed here, after she left Creek House."

Noah hesitates, the big wet fish, so it's me who knocks loudly on the door and fixes a rictus smile on my face in case they answer. But no one comes. It's a nice day – they'll be out enjoying themselves. Noah unlocks the door and we step inside.

"They're very messy," I say. The hall is strewn with sandy, wet towels and footwear, and the sitting room smells of fish and chips because the renters have left their dirty plates on the coffee table.

"You think this is bad – this is nothing," says Noah. "People don't look after it if it doesn't belong to them."

We pick our way through the ground floor with Noah

twitching every time I touch anything. The only landline is in the kitchen. The washing machine is in a small utility room off the kitchen, with no door between them. The cottage has good places to hide – a broom cupboard, a large oak trunk, an old outhouse which holds windbreaks and deckchairs. I go upstairs by myself. Noah doesn't want us both trapped up there if the renters come back. "No one comes back at three o'clock. It's too early on a sunny afternoon," I say. "They'll be out all day." He's beginning to annoy me. He's not really committed to finding Kat.

Upstairs has spacious fitted wardrobes, though these guests prefer to throw clothes in the direction of their suitcase instead. And a large brass bed with an overhanging throw. It would be easy to wriggle under there if you needed to hide in a hurry. The room has blackout blinds and shutters so you wouldn't see from outside if a light was on.

There's a map of the local area on the landing, like the one Nick has in the boot room. I trace the route from Creek House to here with my finger. And back again. I nearly missed it – it's so tiny but unmistakeable. A doodle has been drawn in the field, like it's a genuine symbol used by Ordnance Survey. Two sheep. She couldn't help herself. Exactly like on the map back at Creek House.

"Find anything?" Noah asks, as I join him back by the front door.

"Nothing," I say.

"Mum would have said if there were signs someone had

been in here."

Except his mum knew that Noah had been in Friar's Cottage fixing stuff, cleaning up while her back was bad. If the place wasn't spotless, she'd have put that down to his efforts not being up to her usual standards. I know Kat used the washing machine, that she cleaned up after herself. All this time Noah's been playing CSI and he didn't even know he'd pointed Kat to where she'd stayed for a few days. He told her the key code.

I nod. "Yeah, you're right, Noah. Sorry for dragging you up here. It's a dead end."

Noah looks relieved, talking about how we should stay in touch and share any 'developments in the investigation', as if that's what this is. "Can we meet up later before you have to go tomorrow?" he says. He's a loser, not a winner, in this game. He'll never join the dots between his reams of information and stats and endless photographs. Not when he's scared of the truth.

I zone him out because in my head I'm estimating roughly how many different people must have stayed in this cottage in the intervening year and how many times it will have been cleaned by Noah's mum in her rubber gloves with her love of bleach and disinfectant spray.

And whether there'll be any physical trace of Kat in here for anyone to find at all.

But mostly I'm thinking of Kat. And that she left a sign for me.

10 August 2018

As Kat and I headed back up the drive to Creek House after our night at the pub, a screen was glowing by the front door. Matt was sitting on the doorstep, scrolling on his phone. Kat smirked.

"You really shouldn't have bothered waiting up for us," she said, stepping over him and knocking him with her knee. "Especially as you so obviously need your beauty sleep."

"Nice evening, Millie?" he said, ignoring her. "You missed some epic table football."

"Such a shame to have missed out on a puerile lads' shouting match," said Kat. "Our evening was way more entertaining, wasn't it, Millie?"

The two of them weren't really interested in my replies or whether I was nodding or shaking my head. They were busy glaring at each other and I was collateral damage. I'd already spent an evening sandwiched between Noah and Kat, crunching ice cubes and having nothing to say; being invisible. Whatever Kat said, our evening was *not* entertaining. The best bit was Noah giving us a lift back to the end of the drive and me finding half a packet of fruit pastilles down the side of the seat.

Now I slipped past Matt and waited in the hall. Close enough that I could listen and far enough away that it looked like I couldn't.

"I wasn't expecting you back so early," said Matt. "Your night with the local yokel not go well? I'm sure he's absolutely fascinating. Tell me, Kat; is it jam first or clotted cream with him?"

"He's older than you so I don't expect you to understand higher levels of conversation. You no doubt have been shouting one syllable words like 'Goal' all evening."

"I thought he was a bit young for your tastes these days," said Matt.

"I'm interested in maturity not numbers. I'll probably see Noah again very soon. Very soon indeed."

"Fresh meat is fresh meat, I suppose."

"Luckily, it's abso-bloody-lutely nothing to do with you," she said. "I learned many perfect phrases on my French exchange which would suit you nicely but let's go with 'Espèce d'idiot'."

"Jeez Louise. Whatever. Night night."

They came into the house together but Kat paused by the hall table and turned back. "I might see if Charlie's still awake. He always liked a good bedtime story – something with plenty of secrets and thrills. What do you think, Matt?"

Matt looked up quickly. "Kat. Don't." They held each other's gaze for a moment and then she laughed and threaded her arm through mine.

"Lucky for you, I'm so tired I might go straight to bed." She gave an exaggerated yawn.

"It's a shame we had such a rubbish evening," I said, as

we reached our room.

Kat smiled back at me. "Oh, Millie. What on earth do you mean? I got exactly what I wanted out of it. In several ways."

When I get back to the house, Matt and Charlie are playing table tennis outside. "I've made a start on the bonfire for tonight. What's happening on food?" I ask.

"No idea," says Matt. "Jem and I drove down to the shop, restocked beers and got some bread and stuff. She said she'd sort it later." The boys are in a long rally – Matt tells me all this without taking his eyes off the table. No sign of Jem in the kitchen. Kat is back in my head again, though, just when I thought I was getting better at containing her.

Noah didn't know Kat at all. He thinks he did. He thinks they had something going on for, like, a day and a half, and that gives him the right to keep photos of the two of them. But he didn't have the first idea of what she'd do at Friar's Cottage whereas I could tell exactly. I could practically see her there, plotting away, relishing how clever she was being in her own little hideaway. No one knows her like I do.

I take my time on the stairs. Kat and I worked out the code for the creaky steps and floorboards one wet afternoon when I was about nine. We called it the Kat Burglar game. One of us stood beside the door to our room with eyes tight shut and the other had to sneak up the stairs without her hearing a thing. Make a noise and you lost a life. Kat insisted on nine lives because of her name. I was allowed five. The route back to our room without making a single sound is ingrained, a muscle memory, despite the time gap since playing the game.

I rub the chalk from my hands as though I'm limbering up for a climbing wall. The first step to our floor is the worst so I move on to the second in a giant stride. Next two stairs dead centre, step over the fifth which is a creaky nightmare. Left and left again before contorting myself to land on the top stair on the right-hand side.

Then comes the trickiest bit – the landing. Three strides along the skirting-board edge to the old armchair then a diagonal of baby steps across the rug to reach our room. Silently. Kat would be proud.

I do a double take. *She*'s there. In our room. Facing away, kneeling on the floor by the chest of drawers, her hair up in a towel and wearing a white dressing gown. The back of my neck prickles.

"Kat…?" I say in a whisper. "Kat."

The figure turns. It's not Kat. It's Jem, looking as guilty as hell. Then I realize what she's doing: she's reaching into the drawer where I found the padded envelope.

"Millie! You made me jump. I was looking for something – an old top of mine. It's not at home in London, so I was thinking it could have ended up in the drawers down here."

I half want to say nothing, to watch while she carries on coming out with this convoluted lie. She said too much in a fluster. I wait to see how far she'll dig herself into a hole before I intervene.

"You startled me," I say. "I thought…"

"It is my house, Millie," she says. "I can go in the rooms. We all leave stuff down here. I need it back before the sale."

"Which top?"

"Sorry?"

"Which top are you looking for? I can help you search for it."

"Erm, the one with the clouds on – the blue one. Remember? It's fine. It isn't here."

"The thing is, why would it be in our room – mine and Kat's?" I can see her rising alarm that I'm not playing along with the lie. Kat was right about all those secrets and lies in our families. And that we all know how to bluff.

"In case Kat took it. You know how she borrowed things and never gave them back. And Millie, this isn't *your* room." She moves to go but I take a step, narrowing her route to the door.

"I haven't seen the top." I pause, long enough to see the worry in her eyes before I speak again. "But I did find something else."

She pales.

I reach under my mattress and pull out the package. "It's quite the arts-and-craft project."

I tip the contents on to the floor, spilling out white paper and envelopes, latex gloves, glue and tweezers along with a shower of cut-out words and phrases assembled from magazines and newspapers. Like a mega-mean game of

Scrabble. 'Bitch' 'Are your doors locked?' 'Ugly cow'. I poke them with my toe like they're toxic.

Which I suppose they are.

I'm relieved that it's Jem's, not Kat's. I didn't ever want to believe it was anything to do with Kat. But something in Jem's face, and the tears now rolling down her cheeks, makes me still ask the question:

"Does all this belong to you?"

Dear Kat,

I think some people have something missing.

A dark pit where their heart should be.

A conscience that's completely vanished.

But that will catch up with them one day, right?

If there's any justice in the world.

M xx

11 August 2018

The atmosphere was heavy and close – like we were headed for a storm that needed to break.

Kat had gone for a walk before I was up. I didn't know why she couldn't take me with her rather than leaving me at the whim of the oldies. Mum had insisted on dragging me along with her and Anna through the couple of galleries and gift shops in the village for 'girl time'. Jem had escaped by opting for piano practice while the house was quiet.

We stopped off at the farm shop café on the way back to meet up with Liz. The farm shop sold 'artisan food products' and designer clothing rather than potatoes and cattle feed. It was full of women exactly like Anna, Mum and Liz.

Liz had bought Dom an expensive dark blue jacket. He hung back, looking awkward in the new purchase, as reluctant to join 'the girls' as I was to stay there.

"I might get some shots," he said and headed outside. I wished I had a camera to use as an excuse to escape.

The mums didn't need me to say anything, just chatted away without expecting me to contribute. I licked my finger, picked up all the croissant flakes from my plate one by one and hoped we were leaving soon.

Liz googled the treatment list for the spa at the hotel Rob and Giselle were staying at.

"Here we are: pregnancy journey, three hundred pounds.

'*Harnessing the wisdom of the planet to create magical time for you and your beautiful bump.*' Please! Three hundred quid for a scalp massage and a body scrub."

"Sounds lovely," said Mum.

"It's not lovely at all. *She* is spending money that's mine and the twins' by right."

"How much did you just pay for Dom's jacket?" I asked. My sole contribution to the discussion.

All eyes suddenly turned to me. Mum kicked my foot under the table. "Millie!" she whispered with a shake of her head.

"What? You don't even know if Giselle is having that treatment."

"Of course she'll be having it," spluttered Liz. "Why stay at a spa hotel if you're not going to use the spa!" She had a way of still smiling at me while looking very angry.

"Why don't you walk back to the house, Millie, and see if Kat and Jem are free yet?" said Mum.

Liz replaced her cup in its saucer with a clatter. "They have deliberately chosen a hotel, a *spa* hotel, a couple of miles drive from where they knew *I* would be. What does that tell you?"

I opened my mouth to answer but Mum caught my eye and I shut it again. That was possibly one of those rhetorical questions that they fired off all the time.

Liz dabbed at her lips with the tip of the cloth napkin. "Betrayal is the very worst thing, Millie. I hope you never

212

have to experience it like I have."

"Maybe I will head back," I said and pushed out my chair.

Outside I could instantly breathe easier. I leaned on a fence looking out across the farmland, resting my chin on my hands.

"Isn't it beautiful?" Dom stood beside me with his camera. I hadn't heard him coming. "Are they still talking in there?"

"I'm not very good at chatting," I said. "I seem to say the wrong thing all the time."

"It's easily done," he said. He nodded back in the direction of the café. "High maintenance doesn't even come close." Then put his finger on his lips. "Don't repeat that, will you."

I shook my head. "I'd rather be out here. This is one of my favourite views."

"You have a good eye. Here, take a shot." He held out his camera.

"I don't know how."

"It's digital – it does most of the work for you."

I looked through the viewfinder.

"Choose your angle. What do you want to focus on? Maybe something in the foreground?"

"That hay bale?"

"Cool. Turn the lens until you're happy with it. Bit cloudy today. Here, let me add a filter." He screwed a disc on to the end of the camera lens and handed it back to me. "Try that. Rotate until you get the effect you want."

As I turned the filter, the sky seemed bluer, the clouds

fluffier and whiter.

I clicked the shutter. And again.

"You can make anything better with a polarising filter," he said. "If only we could get something that worked as well in real life."

He told me how to look at the shots I'd taken. They were good, better than the ones I took on my phone where I often accidentally chopped a bit off or had my own shadow butting in. I scrolled back through.

There were photos of Kat. On her own. Smiling or looking up at the lens through her fringe. In one, her head was turned, looking back over her shoulder. He'd captured the light falling through the trees on to her face. She was beautiful.

Dom leaned in to see what I was looking at. "Ah, Liz asked me to get some portrait shots. Update their family photos." He put the camera back round his neck.

Funny how I didn't see any updates of Charlie.

Liz and Anna's laughter drifted over from the doorway. "Looks like they're nearly ready," he said.

"Then I'd better go. I said I was walking back on the footpath. Thanks for letting me try out your camera."

"Pleasure." Dom took off his sunglasses and cleaned them with a cloth from his pocket. A pattern of tiny seagulls rubbing away the smears. "What is it with holidays, Millie? Something about the break in routine, the sunshine, makes everything seem possible. Even mad ideas. Things you wouldn't normally consider."

"All holidays end," I said sharply. "And things go back to how they were. How they should be."

"And I suppose I have to grow up one day," he said, sighing slightly. "But maybe not just yet."

I ran across the field, scattering the birds picking at the crop. I ran until my chest hurt.

The DIY poison-pen-letter kit lies on the floor. New words keep jumping out at me, like cruel Boggle. Jem is still sobbing in a crumpled, towelling heap on my bed. I can't make any sense of what she's saying. I've never seen Jem cry like this and I want her to stop. I pass her some sheets of toilet roll and awkwardly pat her back until finally her sobs turn to sniffs and shudders.

"Who were you sending them to, Jem?" I ask.

She blows her nose and looks up at me with puffy, red eyes. "They're not mine. They're Kat's. I was the delivery person."

"Kat's? What do you mean?"

"She was sending horrible messages to Giselle."

"She wouldn't do that," I say. But I know she would.

Jem leans back against the headboard and wipes her nose again. "Kat gave me a batch of letters when we were here at New Year and asked me – told me – to take them back to London and post them, one a week. Kat didn't want any postmarks from Bristol to show they were coming from her." She sniffs. "She said it was a game with Giselle and her dad."

"A game?"

"But you know how Kat always got bored quickly with any game. After a couple of months she wanted to take it

216

up a notch. She wanted the notes hand-delivered to their house or left where Giselle would find them – on her car windscreen, the bench in the garden. My piano teacher's near their place in Clapham so I could do it before my lesson. I didn't know what was in the envelopes, I swear."

"But you could guess."

She nods. "I knew it wasn't a game. Sometimes my hands were shaking so much after delivering them I couldn't get my fingers under control for my lesson. She sent a new set of letters at the end of July for me to deliver before we all came down here. I opened one of them, and then another and another. I knew they were horrible, deep down I knew. But when I saw it there, in my hand…"

She starts crying again.

"I said it was sick, that I wasn't going to deliver another one."

"But…"

"Kat wouldn't let me stop. She said she'd tell the police it was *my idea*. *I* was the one who'd delivered or posted everything. She was miles away in Bristol."

"But you could have explained," I say.

"I want to do a law degree, become a solicitor. I can't get into any sort of trouble with the police. And what would Mum have thought of me? And Dad – he was best friends with Rob at uni. Kat was clever – she told me she'd say I was obsessed with her dad, that something happened when he and I used to go running in the early mornings that last summer he came here, and I was getting my own back."

"And Rob's proved he likes girls way younger than him," I say. "And he'd be in a heap of trouble if she said that too."

"Exactly. But the bottom line was that it *was* me – not her – delivering them."

No wonder Rob was angry when he turned up here last August. He must have assumed it was Liz when she had work meetings in London. Who else hated Giselle enough? When he'd shouted at Liz that it had to stop, I'd thought he was talking about spending money.

"I know I must sound like an idiot for not standing up to her, Millie, but you know what she was like." Her blotchy face looks across at me, waiting for me to nod. "I was on tenterhooks waiting to hear from Mum and Dad that Rob and Giselle had reported it or for a knock on the door from the police. But nothing happened; nothing was said. I started to relax. I thought Kat would get tired of no reaction and she'd stop. Or I'd be able to talk her out of it while we were all here. Things could go back to normal."

I'd noticed last summer that things between Jem and Kat were strained at times. Kat told me she was being irritating.

Jem reaches for more tissues. "But then Giselle and Rob came that day last summer and she was *pregnant*. I didn't know she was pregnant when we were sending all that stuff, I swear, Millie. She must have been terrified that someone was going to hurt her or the baby. Maybe that's why Rob snapped and finally stormed over here."

"And then Kat flew out of the house and hit him." He must have realized then that it was Kat all along, not Liz. The penny must have dropped for Giselle too that it was Kat doing this terrible thing to her.

Jem wipes another tear away with her sleeve. "The baby changed everything. I said to Kat that there was no way I was doing it again. But Kat was even angrier, wanted to show them. You know what she was like."

Was like.

"And you refused?"

Jem nodded. "And that was what we argued about. I came up to talk to her and she was getting all this new stuff ready – even worse than before. I said I wasn't going to carry on with it and she could do what she liked."

I pick through the final contents of the envelope – coffin pictures and funeral directors' details. "She didn't mean any of this – she couldn't have," I say. "She'd have had second thoughts."

"She did. Or, at least, I think she did. By the day of the party she'd changed her mind. I thought she'd finally seen sense. It was such a relief. She hugged me and said she was sorry for dragging me into it. She said I was right and she'd stop it. Move on."

Did she? Did she say that, Jem?

"I wanted to believe her. I wanted us to go back to being friends," says Jem. "That last-night party was kind of normal, like the old days." She reaches for the envelope and begins to ram the contents back in.

"Now the house is being sold, I had to get rid of all this before anyone saw it. You do believe me, don't you, Millie?"

So, now I know why Jem and Kat argued.

And why Jem might need Kat to disappear. For real.

Dear Kat,

It seems to me that the list of people with a motive for wanting you gone is growing.

You certainly upset a lot of people.

Kindness costs nothing, Kat.

My head is hurting with it all.

I'm beginning to think this is like your favourite film, Murder on the Orient Express – and *spoiler alert* everybody did it?

M x

16 August 2018
Missing: 86 hours

I have a good poker face. It's hard to know what I'm thinking. If you play me at cards, you'll never know if I have a royal flush or a pair of twos in my hand. It can come in useful.

I was able to come off that call from Kat and carry on to the beach and tell the others the 'good' news about the body not being Kat. Without mentioning that she was in fact very OK, call off the dogs (literally). My flushed face and slightly shaking hands were very easily excused by the body news. I didn't tell a bare-faced lie at all. I just didn't mention that I'd spoken to her.

If I'm honest, it was good to have a secret between me and Kat. Us two. She'd chosen *me*. Even if it was to get hold of a load of money, which I had no idea how to do.

We trailed back to the house, Charlie and Matt back in their bromance while Jem was adjusting to the new normal of being stuck with only me. I didn't want to spend any time with Liz and Rob – I was worried that Liz's tears might make me wobble. I left them all together in the kitchen. I have the kind of personality that no one ever notices if I've left a room or not.

I went down the stairs to the cellar to retrieve Kat's bag, terrified that the creaky door or the steps would give me away. There's an old fridge that stopped working years ago that Kat used one summer in her treasure hunt (Clue: Chill out down under). I pulled out the plastic bag squashed to fit in the salad drawer. It contained a small rucksack I hadn't seen before. She'd expressly told me *not* to open it – it was private. But I reckoned Kat gave up any right to privacy when she roped me into this. 'New' Millie didn't have to do every last damn thing that Kat told her to.

I went back to the foot of the stairs and looked up to check there was no one coming down before I unzipped the bag. Inside were a few clothes, new ones I didn't recognise. The tag was still on the jeans. At the bottom was a wallet of cash. More than I'd ever seen rolled up in one place. But she was still asking me to scrape together as much money as I could – *my* money – when she already had plenty.

Running my hands around every zip pocket I found make-up and toiletries, a notebook and pen and her passport. And that white bikini. She was going to go sunbathing on my life's savings while the rest of us cried and looked for her. I took it out and screwed it up into my pocket. She'd have to skip the beach. And there was no way now I was going to give her so much money. She'd spent more on that pair of jeans than I'd ever dream of doing.

Kat had planned it all. She'd planned to go. Down to putting this bag where no one would see it, well away from our bedroom. And she hadn't said a thing to me. The passport meant this was never going to be a couple of days of making us worry while she slept on a beach somewhere locally in Cornwall. Wherever she was going, she wasn't waiting for me. She wasn't asking me to play this game with her.

And I didn't believe she was doing this by herself any more. No one packs that bikini and a load of make-up unless they want to look good for someone.

"Millie – are you coming in?" Mum was shouting for me out in the garden. She liked to know where I was. In fact, I'd be lucky if my parents ever let me go abroad after this – I'd be lucky if they let me go camping in our back garden before I hit thirty. Kat's actions were changing things for all of us. And she didn't care one bit.

I should have taken the bag and given it to Mum or Liz. It was my last chance to tell them about the call, to give them the evidence Kat was alive and well. To tell them about the summerhouse at five.

I'd have been the hero for finding the bag. For finding Kat. For setting a trap to lure her home. I'd have liked to play the hero. Just for one day.

So why didn't I do that? Because I'd promised Kat, because she needed me for once? Because I didn't roll the dice to see what I should do?

I took the bag and hid it in the summerhouse.

I am good at hiding things.

"I don't think it's funny," says Charlie. "Which of you did this?"

He points at the chalkboard in the kitchen. Normally it has something written up like '*Buy garlic*' or a reminder of fish-and-chips night at the pub. But today the whole board is covered with a chalked message:

COMING, READY OR NOT!

It's not only that it's the hide-and-seek words from the last time we all saw her, it's the doodle underneath: a cat's face and whiskers.

She always drew that on birthday and Christmas cards. *Lots of love, Kat* with a cat-face doodle.

Emotions play tricks on you. However much my head was shouting inside that Kat could not have written it, my heart was wishing that she had. That this was all some massive misunderstanding and she was about to emerge from the walk-in larder and say. "Gotcha, guys. Best game of hide-and-seek ever!"

"Matt, I know you like to piss about…"

"I have a sick sense of humour but it wasn't me, Charlie."

They both look at me.

"I wouldn't do that," I say. "Seriously. Why would you think it was me?"

Charlie kicks at the bar stool and it clatters to the floor.

"It's the one-year anniversary tomorrow. Don't mess with my head."

Jem enters the room with her newly dried hair and her eyes still puffy from our conversation. She pulls her buds from her ears and turns to see what we're all staring at. "What the…? Rub it off," she says. She picks up a tea towel and runs it under the tap and wipes at the board. First the words disappear into smudgy, white clouds and then she pauses before the cat face. She rubs hard at the ears, eyes and whiskers and the two-dot nose. The mouth smears and is the last to go. A faint, ghostly impression is all that's left on the board.

Anyone could write that in block capitals and make it look like Kat's writing. And anyone who knew her well, knew about the cat face. The three whiskers added to each side, the pointy ears. It suddenly hits me like a wave knocking the feet out from under me that I'm never getting one of those birthday cards again. My chest is too tight.

"I need some air," I say.

Kat is coming at me from all sides and angles down here. Creek House is becoming overwhelming.

Dear Kat,
  Remember when I said secrets are a burden?
  I've had enough of yours.
  M

I go to the tree, the big horse chestnut, back to where this started. I sit with my back against it, touch the rough bark. I take a moment.

My phone beeps with a message from Noah:

"Meet me at the boathouse?"

At Friar's Cottage he asked me to see him later. I have to add 'closure' with Noah and his investigations to my growing 'closure' list. I don't think he has anything else useful to show me. I got what I needed from the fisherman and the cottage – that Kat planned to go to France. But I still don't know who she was planning on going with. Or if she made it there.

My phone rings and I think it's going to be Noah and answer quickly. "I'm on my way."

"Sorry? Have I got the right number? This is Dominic Crawford."

My fingers tighten on the handset. "Dom? I … I'm at Creek House," I stutter. "It's been a year tomorrow."

"Yes, of course. Terrible. Liz still sends me the occasional email to keep me up to date." His voice moves away from the phone as he calls out: "Two minutes." And then he's back. "Look, I don't want to be rude, but we've got people coming over. What did you want to chat about exactly? I'm not sure how I can help you."

My mind whirs. I'm standing in the garden where Kat disappeared, finally talking to the man I wanted to ask so many questions. And all I can come up with is: "Did you buy Kat a bikini? The white one?"

"A bikini? No. Why would I have bought Liz's daughter a bikini? Did Kat tell you that?"

"Not exactly. But it was something she said. I thought that maybe…" My brain is trying to piece together what she said about it, to remember exactly. "You took lots of photos of her. Of Kat."

"I'm a photographer, Millie. Taking photos is what I do. Especially if I'm asked to. Liz wanted pictures of her daughter. And a good thing too, as she gets a lot of comfort from having them now."

He's confusing me, making himself sound kind and noble.

"You had her headband," I say. "That day at the farm shop, you had Kat's headband in your pocket."

"OK, now this is getting weird. I don't even know what you're talking about. But it's beginning to sound like you're accusing me of something."

"Did … did you go to France together?"

"France? Of course not. Where's this coming from?"

"Or plan to go? Last summer, did Kat think you were going to France with her?"

"No. Why would she or anyone think that? I'm very sad about your friend, and I feel absolutely awful for Liz, but you need to be careful with what you're saying, Millie."

"But Kat said, or hinted that…" I stop, no longer sure of what I should think.

"Kat could be challenging. She was a bit of a fantasist – everyone knew that."

How dare he talk about Kat like that? He didn't know the first thing about her. I've known her all my life.

"Of course, one shouldn't speak ill of the…"

Don't say *dead*. I hold the phone to my chest so I can't hear him for a moment.

"The fact is, your friend Kat liked to play people off against one another. She may have said things to you about me, implied certain things, that honestly…" The signal breaks up slightly but as his voice returns he calls out: "Be there in a minute, babe!"

Who's he talking to?

And suddenly it wouldn't matter. Even if she had gone off with him, it wouldn't matter as long as she was OK.

"Who's babe?" I say.

And the signal cuts out.

Shit, shit, shit.

12 August 2018

Kat was in our room, wafting her newly painted nails in the fresh air from the window. She said: "There you are!" as though I was the one who'd been hard to pin down all day, not her.

"Jem was looking for you," I said.

"She found me. Pass the cigarettes, will you?"

I handed her the crumpled pack and her glittery lighter but I wished she wouldn't smoke. I gave her my best disapproving look. "Have you two fallen out?"

"Something and nothing. All good now. Don't worry – I intend to enjoy our last night together as much as you do." She held up a cigarette but didn't light it.

Our last night already. It had all gone too quickly. I squeezed in next to her on the window seat, staring down at the terrace. Mum and Anna were laying the table ready for the big meal while Nick was chatting to Dom. Seemed like Nick was doing most of the talking while Dom nodded from time to time. When Nick took a call and wandered off across the grass shouting into his mobile, Dom turned away looking relieved. He stood with one foot on a chair and a hand on his hip. "Looks like he's modelling for one of those catalogues that fall out of the Sunday papers," I said.

"You are so right, Millie. Exactly that. I'll tell him later. He could get a job selling loafers to the over-sixties."

"Still, Dom has made it through the week. Maybe this

one's a keeper for your mum?"

"Oh, Millie. You're not very good at reading body language, are you? He obviously can't wait to get away. He's only hanging around to make sure he gets a couple of souvenirs courtesy of Mum's credit card, and some good landscape photographs to sell."

Kat stretched her arms above her head and stood up. She looked at herself in the long mirror and adjusted her sunglasses which were holding her hair back, perched on her head. "We should finish getting ready. There isn't much time left."

She seemed ready to me. She was wearing a short blue-and-white striped dress and a green denim jacket. Her make-up was already perfect and her hair straightened.

"Last night, Mills." She sighed. "Want me to help you with what to wear? Or do your nails?"

"Sure." It was like the old days, previous summers, rather than the stress and arguments of this week. Maybe the party would be as good as other years. Maybe a good night tonight would make everything OK again. I laid out two of my dresses on the bed as she lined up the nail polish. She picked up a die from the china bowl of bits and pieces on the chest of drawers and held it up to me.

"If you took every decision on the flip of a coin or a roll of the dice, instead of on your gut, do you think it would work out better, Mills?" She rolled the die between her palms and it clicked against her rings. "From tiny things like what

230

colour to paint your nails to all the big important things in life. If you left that to the dice, to fate, physics, God – whatever you believe in – would life be easier?"

I shrugged. "I'll go for 'Ballet Slippers' not 'Mystère de Minuit'." I pointed to the paler bottle of nail polish.

"Odds or evens?" she said, more to herself. "Odds or evens, Kat?" She walked across the room to the window again, biting her lip, and then back to me.

She threw the die on to the chest of drawers and it settled by the hair straighteners. Six little dots.

"Evens! In that case, Mills, looks like you get to keep it." She tossed me the bottle of polish. "*Voilà.* The die is cast. Fate has told me what to do." She paused a moment then clapped her hands together. "Right, let's get ready."

Dear Kat,

I thought he gave it to you and you really shouldn't have paraded it in front of all of us.

I had to take it because I couldn't bear to see you cheapen yourself.

I knew you'd thank me one day (OK, so I was wrong about that!)

I hid it – all this time. I zipped it into a cushion on the landing – the lumpy, faded blue roses one on the armchair that no one ever sits in.

It was such a tiny amount of material that it barely made

a bump.

But I didn't know then that Anna would find buyers for Creek House and that all these old cushions and furniture would be headed for a skip.

So it's lucky that I'm here. That I came to take it back.

M

I tap at the phone, moving across the garden to get a better signal. I need to get Dom back on the line.

My fingers slip and I can't think how to work the keypad, even though I've used it a million times. Finally, my head clears enough to press 'Recents'. Three rings seem to last an eternity, then Dom answers.

"Is that you, Millie, again?"

"Who's the babe in the background?" I say breathlessly.

"What?"

"Can I speak to her?"

"You want to speak to my fiancée? Why? No!"

"I want to speak to her."

Right now it's what I want most in the world.

His voice goes fainter again. "It's fine, nothing to worry about."

"Is she there?" I say. And again: "Is *she* there?"

"I know you've had a rough year, Millie. But really, this isn't on. I think it's best if we end the call now. Our guests will be here any minute."

"If you don't let me speak to her, I'll keep ringing," I say. "What will your friends make of that?" My voice quivers.

"Give me the phone," says a female voice in the background. And then loud and clear: "Hello. This is Sara Hashim. Hello?"

I don't know her voice at all.

I thought I was going to know her voice.

This woman, Sara, whispers with Dom while I say nothing. It's like I'm down a big dark hole. I don't have any words left.

Dom comes back on the line and says firmly: "We're going to hang up now, Millie. Are you going to be OK? Do you have someone there with you?"

"Yes," I say quietly.

"Good. I think it's best if you don't call us again."

"I… Sorry."

"Don't worry about it. It's obviously an upsetting time around the anniversary. Take care." He rings off and I'm left shaking. And thinking what a fool I just made of myself.

I'm completely losing the plot. I don't know what to think any more.

*

I take my time on the way to the boathouse, trying to make sense of it all. And wishing I'd never started this.

When I get there, Noah's waiting for me on the step outside and leaps to his feet as I arrive.

"Did you come up with something new?" he asks. His face falls as I shake my head. I don't want to tell him about my humiliating call with Dom. All the terrible things he said about Kat.

"I'm sorry I haven't been much use," I say. "My best bet is still that she went to France and your mate didn't want to tell us."

"Chris isn't my mate."

"We'll never know the truth," I say. "I thought Friar's Cottage might have been a good spot to wait for the boat. But no sign of her."

"It's only another theory. There's nothing to help me. Nothing to stop people pointing a finger at me."

"It's a good thing we didn't find anything at Friar's Cottage. As you said, that would be a link between you and Kat for the police to latch on to," I say. "Best not to mention the cottage at all." Kat left a sign that only I would know about. She left that sign for me, no one else.

He nods, his forehead creased up with worry lines. "They'd scapegoat me with any circumstantial evidence, given half a chance."

"Then don't ever give them half a chance," I say. I pull the photos of him and Kat out of my pocket. I've been keeping them flat in my notebook. "I'll run these back upstairs."

"I can do that," he says, holding out his hand.

"It's OK. I'd like to go in for one last time. Sounds stupid, I know, but I'd like to say goodbye to it all. Charlie keeps talking about us finding a way to move on, for our own good, our own mental health. To move on without ever knowing what happened." I'm nervous, speaking too quickly. I don't want him to come up with me.

"I get it," he says. "I need to find a way to do that too."

I don't believe he will. I give him a quick, awkward hug.

"My mum and dad would say we both need to get a hobby," I say, pulling away. "A normal one."

Noah smiles. "Yeah, maybe."

I run up the stairs and take the photo I want. I have more right to it than Noah does. She's wearing that bikini so he really shouldn't have it on his wall. Kat is smiling out at me under the brim of her hat like we're back sharing secrets together.

When I come back down, Noah's at the edge of the beach, skimming pebbles into the water. "If ever you're back down here…" he says, but doesn't finish his sentence. "Anyway, you've got my number to stay in touch, to keep me posted."

"Sure. Definitely I'll be in touch if I hear anything at all." We have an uncomfortable moment of staring at our feet.

He picks another pebble and rubs it between his hands before sending it dipping and skimming across the creek.

"I should get going," I say. "We're having a gathering down on the beach later, so…" Neither of us are any good at finishing our sentences or saying what needs to be said. I leave him as he skims more stones, on his own, and I go back to build up the fire on our own beach for tonight.

*

I take a moment in the garden before I go back to the others. I've got more messages from Mum and Dad checking I'm OK and looking forward to having me home again. They've managed to only mention my impending exam results once.

My finger hovers on the Instagram icon and I can't resist checking @Livresque_KB.

She just won't leave me alone.

A picture of a horse chestnut tree has been added with a single sentence:

1 day, 2 days... 365 days!! Coming, ready or not!!!

#cache-cache #hideandseek #KatsHaveNineLives

Dear Kat,

Tomorrow you'll have been missing for a year. I suppose that makes this 'Anniversary Eve' if that's not too macabre (another of my new favourite words).

I'm making a bonfire down on the beach. I think Anniversary Eve deserves a ceremony. Don't you?

Remember how we used to have a bonfire every New Year? All those special things we did. They were special to me, but I'm learning that they weren't so meaningful to everyone else. To you. That last bonfire there was an atmosphere I was too naïve to pick up on among the adults. But I think you explained it to me last summer in the woods.

Mum brought sparklers. You probably thought it was

childish of me to want them. You probably made a mean comment.

But I liked the sparklers. I liked the fizzing and the way I could write in the dark with the sparks. If I moved my wrist very quickly, I could make shapes that hung there, suspended and beautiful.

Ephemeral. I like that word too. Ephemeral.

Anything I drew or wrote with the sparkler dangled in the air and disappeared. It existed for a fraction of a second.

I dared to make a heart shape, I dared to write a name.

But it was ephemeral. It was gone before it existed.

M

"Finally, you're back," says Matt. "We were about to send out a search party." He glances at Charlie. "Oops. Sorry, mate, I didn't think."

"The bonfire's ready for tonight," I say. "Down on the beach, like we used to do."

"Fab. Kat would have loved that," says Jem, and hugs me. I am her new best friend. For tonight, anyway.

"We're playing a game first. And no, not hide-and-seek ever again," says Charlie. "I had a light-bulb moment and this is the only way for me to move on. Come with me."

We follow him to the TV room. He plonks down in the middle of the floor. Jem sits beside him and puts her hand on his arm.

"I think we've all had enough of games," she says. "There have been way too many of them."

"This is one we've never played before. I invented it," says Charlie. He finishes the beer in his bottle and places it on the floor in front of him. "It's a variation on Spin the Bottle or Truth or Dare." He gestures to the space next to him for me to sit down.

"I think I'll skip it," I say. I yawn. "Actually, it's been quite a long day and if we want to go down to the beach…"

"Sit down," says Charlie, pulling at my leg, making me sink to the floor. "Everyone has to play or it's no fun at all.

239

It's hashtag last-night party time, remember! And you're the one who likes games, Millie."

I don't like games any more. I stopped playing them a year ago.

I sit cross-legged between Jem and Charlie, and Matt takes his place opposite me. Charlie's game is already looking like a new ordeal.

"First up: the rules. If the bottle points at you, you have to tell the truth about you and Kat."

"Sounding like a teenage girl sleepover party. I'm out," says Matt.

Jem pokes him. "Try harder not to be a sexist pig."

"No one is allowed to sit out," says Charlie, fixing him with a death stare. "You were right, Millie, that we owed it to Kat to remember her properly, to get to the truth about what happened, to open the box; however you want to put it. A couple of days back here has made me see that." He flicks the bottle to start it spinning. "My new game's called Revelations. Because between us we must know more about what happened to my sister."

The bottle slows down and stops at Jem.

"I didn't have anything to do with it," she says and kicks the bottle gently away with her foot.

"We're after the truth tonight so we get that closure you talked about, Jem. So you have to play. Tonight's our last chance," says Charlie. "And what's said at Creek House, stays at Creek House."

"Steady on," says Matt. "No one's saying any of *us* had anything to do with Kat's disappearance, are we?"

"We were all together. We were all looking for her," says Jem.

Matt shakes his head. "Actually, we weren't all together during the game. We were hiding individually – except for Millie who was clear for anyone to see counting by the tree."

"Until she stopped counting," says Charlie. "Then she was creeping round the dark garden like any of us."

"What? I found you all – one by one," I say.

"Not as fast as you normally do. And what were you doing in between?" says Matt.

"*You* could have done something to Kat while I was counting and then moved her body later while I was in the house looking for her," I say.

Jem shudders. "Is that what you think? That one of us bumped Kat off in the middle of the game?"

"*I* don't think that. It would have been impossible," I say. "But apparently Matt does."

"Impossible is a big word. What did you count to anyway? Fifty?" asks Charlie.

"It was one hundred," says Jem.

"Twenty," I say. "Definitely."

"No, it was quicker than that," says Matt. "Ten?"

"It's hard to remember everything," I say.

"Yes. Sometimes I worry I won't remember what my own

241

twin looks like," says Charlie.

"Lucky for you she made sure there are a gazillion photographs of her," says Matt. Jem pokes him again. "Hey! It needed saying."

"Maybe I need to make myself clearer when I say between us we must know more about what happened," says Charlie. "I think all of us have a place, deep down, that we're ashamed of, where we're glad she's gone. Why would *you* have wanted her to go? I think that's how we see what was really going on last summer."

Matt throws up his hands. "OK. Enough of this psychological claptrap. I know it's hard coming back here, mate, especially as tomorrow's the twelfth, but you are way out of order. None of us wanted to get rid of her."

Charlie rotates the bottle back to Jem. "I think Kat just walked out of our lives. While Millie was counting to whatever it was. But we *all* did things that pushed her into going. We need to own up to them. I think that's the only way we move on. Enough lies and falsehoods. Enough pretending that my sister was a saint."

"She was far from that," says Jem quietly.

"See. Now we're making progress," says Charlie. "You've gone very quiet, Millie. Honesty. That is how we play this game and come out the other side."

Jem looks across at me and sighs. "OK, I'm in. But there has to be a new rule: no consequences, no recriminations."

Charlie puts his hand on his heart. "Agreed. Promise. No

comeback. You two?"

"Agreed," I say with a frown. "But that doesn't mean I think this is a magic wand to make us all feel great." Charlie's not really giving us much of a choice.

"Matt?" Charlie nudges his friend.

"See, you say no recriminations now but…"

"I mean it," says Charlie. "It's not like any of you have got anything terrible to say, is it? I'll start." He turns the bottle to face himself and clears his throat. "She hated that I'd been seeing Dad and Giselle and that I knew about the baby."

"That's hardly a revelation, is it? We know: we were there," says Matt.

"Yeah, but I'd been seeing them for ages. I knew they were going to stay nearby at that hotel. I was going to visit them there. And, way back, more than a year before, I'd seen them together, kissing the face off each other outside a café, before he finally told Mum. Maybe if I'd said something it wouldn't have turned out the way it did with everyone at each other's throats."

"That's on your dad, not you," says Jem.

"I like to think Kat would have come round – especially after Jackson was born. I guess we'll never know. But I did sneak around behind Kat's back seeing Dad. And we were always arguing about him. I said terrible things I regret now." Charlie puts his head in his hands. "I was pissed off about my sports tour to South Africa being canned so there

243

was more money to pay for her fancy sixth form. I said it would be easier for everyone if she wasn't here at all."

"That's pretty normal brother/sister stuff, mate," says Matt. "In my limited experience."

"But I meant it. I *really* meant it. I'd hate to think that was the lasting memory she had of me."

Jem lays a hand on his arm. "It wouldn't have been."

"And it became true. Like I'd wished it," he says quietly.

He sits back for a moment or two with his head bowed while I hope the game is over.

But Charlie leans forward and spins the bottle again. "Time for the next player."

It winds up pointing to Jem. "Here goes." She swallows hard. "Kat was making me deliver malicious notes to Giselle. They were foul and I wanted to stop and as soon as I realized Giselle was pregnant I did, for good. Kat and I had a massive falling-out over it."

Charlie raises an eyebrow and lets out a low whistle. "I knew Kat hated her, but I didn't think she'd do something like that. Dad never said."

"He probably didn't want to make matters worse," says Jem.

"Wow. Imagine someone hating you that much. When you've got a baby on the way too," says Matt.

"Kat was so irrational about anything to do with Giselle. It was scary," says Jem.

"So, now we're getting somewhere. Thank you, Jem, for

your honesty." Charlie squeezes her hand. "See, this is how we all feel better. This is how we see what was really going on. Why Kat would want to run out of here, away from all of us." His mouth's locked in a grim smile.

The bottle twirls and stops at Matt this time. "I don't know if this is a good idea," he says. He reaches behind him for his beer and takes a couple of mouthfuls.

"We all agreed to play the game," says Charlie.

"I did it," says Jem. "It's your turn."

Matt looks down at his hands. And speaks quietly. "Don't say I didn't warn you. Kat and I hooked up together."

Charlie's smile evaporates. "What do you mean?"

"At New Year. It was dumb. I regretted it. It was all wrong time, wrong place, and one thing led to another."

"You too!" says Jem. "That was never going to end well."

"I assumed it meant nothing to her too, but I was wrong about that," says Matt. "She wanted it to carry on when we were back here last summer. She was … intense. That's why I kept wanting to go to the beach, to be in big groups, to not get stuck on my own with her at Creek House."

"You and Kat?" says Charlie, slowly, like his brain can't compute it. "You and my sister?"

"She liked the sneaking around. All that flirting with gawky Noah was designed to make me jealous. And Liz's boyfriend too. Even though it was plain he saw her as a little kid. It was like she was playing us all off against each other, with her as the prize. I was tempted – she made it *very* tempting. But I really didn't want the prize any more – and she went nuts about it."

"Like I said – never going to end well," says Jem. "What an idiot. Why couldn't you keep it in your trousers the first time?"

"She threatened to tell you, but I'm guessing she didn't, mate?" says Matt. "Lucky that we all agreed no recriminations, hey?"

Charlie puffs out his cheeks and tucks his hands under his thighs. Probably to stop himself hitting out.

"And there's something else," says Matt. "It's probably nothing, but Kat asked me who I was getting my pot from down here. I pointed him out one day – this fisherman called Chris. I don't know if she went ahead and bought anything off him. She and I weren't exactly on best buddy terms for the rest of the week."

At least that explains how Kat linked up with Chris. This game of Charlie's is joining up the dots for me.

"And you didn't think to mention this to the police?" asks Charlie.

"I thought she was curious about where I was getting it in a tiny place like this – I didn't see her smoking any. She could have got it off me if she was actually interested. I honestly didn't think it was relevant."

"And you *so* didn't want to get yourself into trouble," says Jem.

"Millie – your turn," says Matt quickly. He pushes the

bottle over to me. "What had Kat done to you, beyond the usual way she treated you like her personal lapdog?"

"Why would you have wanted her to go, hypothetically?" asks Jem.

I run my tongue over my dry lips. "She'd blown her GCSEs," I say. "I think she wanted to leave before that came out."

"We know that. We got her results," says Charlie. "Obviously, Mum and Dad didn't care at all in the grand scheme of their daughter missing."

"Failing exams is a reason for Kat to choose to go," says Jem. "But what did she do to you, Millie, to make you want her to leave?"

All eyes are turned on me.

I don't like this game.

I formulate sentences in my head. *I thought we were going to be friends forever; I thought we'd go travelling together; she left me in the window seat when I was six; she pushed me away; she threw herself at people who didn't love her; she ruined things.*

They all sound stupid reasons. Childish. Not enough of a motive to kill someone. Not enough for the big reveal at the end of an Agatha Christie book.

I start to cry. Fat tears that fall down my cheeks and sobs that shake my chest. Charlie puts his arm round my shoulders but that only makes it worse.

"She didn't take me with her," I say. "She didn't *want* to take me with her."

Dear Kat,

Within me lies a never-ending game of hide-and-seek.

I needed you to write back – even if it was only a cat face and one line on the noticeboard.

Cache-cache.

Amelia

12 August 2018

"I thought we were going to play games," I said. "Before there's any dancing."

"Ever thought about opening up your own board-game café, Millie?" said Matt. "Then you'd have an endless stream of people who share your obsession."

"Games! Yes, let's," said Kat in a silly, little-girl voice. She opened the games cupboard wide. "Escape from Colditz, Ticket to Ride? Pandemic – way too far-fetched and depressing. What do you think, Matt – up for a game of Frustration? Or look, Jem – that Love Letter game is a quick one. Codewords? Scrabble? Or, Charlie, how about an epic game of Risk?"

The others were scowling. But I was beaming. Finally.

Kat turned to face us all, her arms crossed. "Maybe we go old school and play Consequences, Truth or Dare? Or good old Happy Families? You decide, brother dearest."

"Give it a rest, Kat," said Charlie. He'd cycled over to his dad's hotel earlier that afternoon and Kat was still fuming. Charlie threw a Frisbee over to Matt, hitting the lampshade. "Garden?"

"Sure, I could do with the fresh air," said Matt. "Jem? Millie?"

"No … wait," I started, but they were already going out. "It's always better with more of us playing."

"Sorry, Millie. Another time." Jem left too and joined the

boys throwing that stupid plastic disc around like a bunch of Labradors playing fetch.

Kat was smiling like she'd won something but somehow she'd ruined my evening. She knew how much I'd been looking forward to it and she'd put the others off.

"Lightweights," she said. "Oh, Millie, don't look so sad." She hugged me, and I breathed in the smell of lemony shampoo. "It's good to have you all to myself at last. The days are flying by. We could play a game for two. Backgammon, Carcassonne? Anything but chess, you know I don't have the patience for it."

"Thank you," I whispered.

She released the hug and held me by both shoulders, looking me straight in the eyes. "And I'll make them all join in later – what's the one game you want us all to play?"

I looked at the board-game cupboards and I thought about all the years of coming here and how things were changing. I couldn't guarantee we'd all be together again at New Year or next summer. I wanted to play the one game that I had the best memories of, the one I'd always enjoyed the most. The one I planned for and strategized over. The one that Creek House with its beautiful, quirky gardens was made for.

I didn't hesitate: "Hide-and-seek."

Charlie was right. I feel better, everyone seems to feel better, for playing his game. Even if I cheated. My hand tightens around the notebook of letters in my pocket. There's no need for me to share them with the others and spoil the atmosphere. We've had quite enough truth for one evening.

I don't know that the boys will be best buddies again immediately after Charlie learning what Matt was up to with his sister, but maybe they'll work through it in their own way with a game of Frisbee and a kickabout.

Jem can go on and be a hotshot lawyer without a blemish to her name. Only to her conscience. And she's pretty good at ignoring that already. Charlie will play with his half-brother on weekends and never call him anything he might regret. Maybe one day he'll confirm to Giselle those letters were down to Kat. And she'll be relieved, not for the first time, that Kat has disappeared.

It's our last night at Creek House. Our last night ever. And we all have ghosts to lay to rest.

We light my bonfire down on the beach. Jem throws in the package from our room, and we watch as those nasty words of Kat's shrivel and burn for good.

The boys get me and Jem to whoop and dance around the fire like we did when we were seven. We finish the beer and the wine and the crisps. I'm glad my head is so fuzzy.

Charlie says it's his last drink and we all want to believe him.

We lie on blankets on the beach as the air chills and watch a shooting star skip across the sky. We listen for owls like we did when we were little kids.

We are the only people on the face of the earth.

It's a party of a kind, but one with tears and laughter.

I've never felt so much a Creeker as tonight.

I know the hiding places better than anybody.

The window seats in the summerhouse have faded box cushions with red and white stripes. The picture window has the largest, and it's not just a seat. If you throw off the cushions and lift the lid, this is where the croquet set used to be stored, years ago. Kat put me in there one year when I was little. She closed the lid on me, giggling. I was excited to have such a good spot to hide. At first.

She told me to stay there until she returned – that was the game. But she left me, rammed in, for ages. By the time she came back for me and hooked me out, I was a shaking, sobbing mess. And I'd wet myself. Kat held her nose at the smell. But I didn't tell on her. I should have done, but I'd promised not to, cross my heart and hope to die.

The old garden furniture was stacked inside the summerhouse, faded and broken. I sat on one of the cane chairs and waited, pulling at a thread on my cuff. The oldies were out. There was an update at five at the police station. Mum had suggested they have a final walk along the coast path to decompress afterwards and 'clear away the cobwebs' before we all drifted off home. Matt and Jem had offered to finish shutting down the house, and Charlie was out cycling to burn off his anger and make one last search of the area.

All Kat needed to do was skirt around the edge of the

holly at the back of the garden and reach the summerhouse. She wasn't as good as me at sneaking about the place. She likes to be seen way too much to ever be good at blending into the background. But all those years of hide-and-seek and forty-forty-in would pay off.

I had her bag ready in the hiding place with the extra money she'd asked for. I'd taken notes from Mum's purse. There wasn't much in there – no one uses cash these days. And I'd taken some money out of my bank account, but not all of it. Not as much as I knew she wanted. I'd had to go down to the village with Dad and I got flustered because he was literally on the other side of the shop and could have come over at any moment. There was a stupidly low limit on the amount I could take out of my account in one go but it was better not to give her loads anyway – she already had plenty of money in her bag. If she needed more, she'd have to come back. And I could persuade her to stay and give all this up.

Unless someone else was helping her too.

The door shuddered open and Kat came in, hood up, slightly out of breath. "Forty-forty-in," she said, smiling and slapping the door like we used to do. "No one saw me."

I stared at her, part-ghost, part-real-life flesh and blood. I'd thought I'd never see her again.

But here she was. Her cheeks flushed and her eyes bright as though this was a game from when we were younger.

She hugged me and I clung to her back, breathing in the

familiar smell of her before she pulled away. "Oh, Mills, did you miss me?"

I nodded and blinked back a tear. I waited for her to say she'd missed me too and it had all been a terrible mistake.

But she didn't.

"Though it would have been better if you'd brought the bag to me, like I asked," she said. "Did you get some more money?"

"Why do you need it?" I asked. "Where are you going?" My voice sounded brittle and dry.

"Where is it?" she said looking behind me.

"I put it in the hiding place. You know, the one only you and I know about." I gestured to the window seats.

"Fancy you remembering that," said Kat. "Hope the smell's died down." She pushed off the cushions and pulled out her bag. She checked the cash. "Is this *all* the extra you got?"

"I took all I could out of my account and I *stole* the rest," I said. "I stole it. For you."

"You sound angry, Mills. I thought you wanted to help me. It's all been a bit…"

"Complicated?" I said. "It's complicated here too. Awful, in fact. Your mum and Charlie are going back to Bristol tonight in case you turn up there."

"And Dad?"

"He's driving back to London tonight. With Giselle."

She stopped at the mention of Giselle.

"And the bump," I added as she grimaced. I paused as I looked properly at her, trying to fix an image in my head. The same time yesterday, I'd thought I'd never see her again. And now she was back. Briefly. And then I'd lose her all over again.

She sat on the edge of one of the broken cane chairs. It creaked and dust rose up, captured in the sunlight, like glitter. She looked tired.

For a moment I thought she was going to relent, call an end to it all.

"It's not too late to sort this out," I said.

"It is too late. At first I wasn't sure, but now I know this is what I want. I'm not backing out now." She grabbed my hands. "*Je ne regrette rien*, remember, Mills."

"But where are you going?" I wanted to ask her to take me with her. I wanted to say that I didn't care where we were going or how much trouble we'd be in, as long as she took me with her.

She sighed. "Will you stop asking me that, please? Stop going on and on. Nagging me. If I don't tell you, you won't be able to tell anyone else. You were always rubbish at the Yes-No question game."

"I wasn't. You don't trust me…"

"I'm sorry, Millie," she snapped, in that way she had of showing the discussion was over. There was that word again: *sorry*. But she sounded anything but sorry. She drew her hair back and piled it at the nape of her neck before fastening her hairclip. I took a step back towards the door. I was suddenly hot. The sunshine was streaming in through the glass on to my face and the strong smell of the little white flowers climbing up the sides of the summerhouse was making me queasy.

"Please, Kat…" I began.

She sighed heavily. "I really don't have time to deal with this right now. Are we done?" Kat zipped up the bag and tucked her hair back into her hood. It was too hot for a hood. My head was filling with stupid, irrelevant thoughts like that, when I needed to find the words to make her stay.

I didn't know what I'd expected from this meeting, but this wasn't it. Wasn't I meant to be the guardian angel helping her out? She hadn't even said thank you for bringing the bag, for stealing money for her, for not telling anyone. People should always say thank you.

"I'll get in touch when I'm settled. You have to promise me, Mills, that you won't say anything."

"I could say something in a few days' time – to let them know you're OK."

"No. It's my decision, Millie. I'll get in touch when the time's right. Say nothing." This time she gripped me by the wrist so tight it hurt. "Promise me!"

I nodded. "I promise," I whispered. "Cross my heart."

"And what?"

"Hope to die." I drew a cross on my chest with my finger, like she used to make me do when we were younger.

A banging noise coming from the garden made us both jump.

"What's that?" She stood behind me. "Isn't everyone out of the way? You said they were."

"They are. The oldies are all in town. Anna gave Jem and Matt jobs to do before we leave. Charlie's out on his bike. I suggested it."

"I can't have anyone find me, Millie. I knew this was a stupid risk coming back to Creek House." She looked panic-stricken. A scaredy-Kat. "See who it is. Get rid of them."

"I'll go and check. Don't worry. No one comes to the summerhouse," I said. I stopped, my hand on the door frame. "If it's not safe to go out the way you came in, I'll come straight back and tell you."

I lifted the lid on the window seat and put her bag back in. "You should hide," I added. "Just for a few minutes to make sure. The bag's like a cushion, make it more comfortable."

"Hide in there? It's tiny. You have to be kidding me?"

"Better safe than sorry. Do you want to be found or not?"

The banging started up again. Charlie's voice boomed across the garden.

"Well?"

This was an even worse goodbye than I'd anticipated. No hug, no tearful farewell. It was going to end like this – with Kat glaring at me.

"It'll be fine," I said. "I'll distract him. Wait a few minutes and go."

She climbed in. "I said you should have brought the bag to me."

I looked down at her.

There was so much I wanted to say but she was already curled up and complaining. "Get a move on, Millie. Keep him out of the way."

"Bye, Kat. Take care."

I lowered the lid and her mumbled words were muffled.

That was it. Bye. So long. Adieu. Farewell.

I hurried through the garden back to the lawns and the sound of Charlie's voice. He was with Matt and Jem, manhandling the angel statue and swearing loudly.

"What are you doing? I thought you were out on your bike."

"Puncture before I even got past the farm shop."

"Anyway, we need his muscles to help my puny brother with this," said Jem. "We're moving Angelina Jolie. Mum said she doesn't want to look at a broken angel."

"It *is* like something from a scary *Doctor Who* episode," said Matt.

Charlie stood up a moment and rested his hands on his hips. "I did break it, so…"

"Mum doesn't care about that. But St Angelina is now too far on the shabby side of shabby chic to fit with her decoration scheme," said Matt. "Plus, Mum and Jem think it's bad luck, like smashing a mirror."

"Don't mock; it is," said Jem. "And we don't want any more bad luck around here. Don't forget this." She dragged the broken wing out of the plants.

"Even now we've bashed her off the plinth, Angelina is heavier than she looks," said Matt, stopping again to wipe his forehead. "We need to shove her out of sight somewhere she can't give my sister the evil eye."

"Put her in the big yew," I suggested. "I'd like to have her in there. Watching over me."

I looked back across the garden. Kat would be fine, able to get away without them seeing her.

"I've been looking for my book. I thought I might have left it somewhere out here," I said, answering a question they hadn't asked me.

"Please don't smash up any more statues, mate," said Matt. "Pick something smaller and lighter next time it's all too much."

I wanted to scream out that Kat wasn't worth all the angst, wasn't worth caring about. Not worth destroying things over. Not worth looking for. That two minutes ago they could have had a whole conversation with her in the summerhouse.

I wanted to tell them she'd *chosen* to leave me, and them.

"Are you all right, Mills?" asked Jem.

"Yes. It's weird to be going home while Kat's still out there somewhere. But Dad has to work and…"

"It's OK. You've been brilliant," said Charlie. He forced

himself to smile. "We're heading back to Bristol anyway in case she turns up there. And Mum thinks I should be around to get my GCSE results. Though who cares about that now, right?"

I hadn't been 'brilliant'. Not at all. I'd been a double-crossing, lying worst-friend-ever. Charlie looked so sad.

I opened my mouth to say something. To say: if you run, you'll catch her heading through the woods. Charlie, run. Now!

But my promise to Kat stopped me. I opened and closed my mouth like a guppy again. "I'd better finish packing," I said.

"Set up some cold drinks for us, Mills," said Matt.

Kat's stupid game was making me want to get as far away from my beloved Creek House and the Creekers as possible. Away from all the lies.

Kat had ruined everything.

Every last thing I cared about.

Dear Kat,

Fanfare This is the last letter.

It's been a blast, but all good things must come to an end. Everyone's talking about closure.

I did what the counsellor told me to do. I am such a good girl.

But these letters were only ever for me and you. For no one

261

else. I am very good at hiding things. I think I've proved that, right from the beginning. It's my special talent and it turns out to be a lot more useful than any of the ones I used to envy in you and the other Creekers.

And I'm not sure that everyone would like what I've written, and they might misinterpret certain things.

I might get into trouble.

And that wouldn't be fair.

Sorry. Not sorry.

It's been cathartic. (I like that word and how it uses all my mouth to say.) It's given me a chance to think over what happened, and my part in it.

Guilt and regret are powerful.

That phrase of yours from the Edith Piaf song (I looked it up) – Je ne regrette rien.

I don't think it's quite right. We all regret stuff. Mistakes, errors, plans that didn't work out exactly the way we wanted them to. Unintended consequences. That ripple effect from the stone in the pond Mum showed me.

Do you regret asking me, Kat?

Of all the Creekers you could have picked, you chose me. Dependable, puppy dog Millie-Moo.

That would be something to regret.

Je ne regrette rien.

Amelia Thomas

12 August 2019
Missing: One Year

My bag's packed and stowed in the car. Charlie's going to give me a lift to the station. Jem and Matt are piling up their boot with anything they want to keep and take back to London themselves. They won't be down here again before the sale goes through and the removers come.

It's the end of Creek House.

But everyone is lighter. Kinder to each other.

"One last walk around the garden?" I say to Charlie.

"Sure." He takes the flowers from the vase. "We can put these by the conker tree. For Kat. The anniversary."

The grass is damp with dew and we leave footprints as we cut across the lawn. The day is going to be warm. It's full of promise.

Charlie crouches down and takes great care to prop up the flowers against the trunk. For a moment I expect him to say a few words or a prayer as he's so still.

"Kat would like that," I say. "White roses were her favourite." I knew her best.

He stands again, takes my hand and squeezes gently. He smiles. Like the *old* Charlie.

I said goodbye to the beach last night. I haven't done the summerhouse. I pull Charlie towards it. The paint's peeling and a couple of the panes are cracked. Maybe summerhouse was always a grander name than it deserved. Now I'm leaving Creek House for good, I'm seeing how run-down it's become. The jasmine climbs across the frame, creating a pungent scent, and tendrils of ivy wind through the roof tiles.

"The garden's taking it over," says Charlie. He pushes aside the brambles, rubs at the dirty glass and peers inside. "Very Gothic. Especially with that angel statue. We dragged it in there last year before we left for home. Remember? Looks like they never got round to fixing it."

I don't hear any more of what he says.

I remember.

Of course, I remember.

My voice has shrunk. "I thought you were putting St Angelina under the yew tree."

"Jem said no, we'd still be able to see her from the house. And she'd be able to see us with her bad-luck stare." He makes a face. "The summerhouse was better – the mausoleum of unwanted things."

"How long did it take you to get it in here from the garden?" I ask in a low voice.

"Don't know. Once Matt put his back into it, it wasn't too bad between us. I can't remember – five minutes? Ten?"

The statue lies serene. The hands still clasped together in prayer. Like a toppled gravestone.

She would have left before the statue was placed there, wouldn't she? She would have shouted out if they'd trapped her in there, wouldn't she?

"Just a pile of junk now," says Charlie, heading back towards the house. "I'll let you say your last goodbyes, Millie. You've got a train to catch."

My mouth's dry. I stare at the window seat, half hidden by the statue.

Was she waiting for me to come back? Then – and now?

The door isn't locked, but stiff. It shudders open, the bottom dragging on the floor. The sickly smell of jasmine mixed with the stale air is overpowering. The heavy statue is propped across the window seat, ramming it shut. The wing rests on the pile of faded red-and-white striped cushions on the ground. I don't know if Kat would have put the cushions back in place when she left. *If* she left, or not.

All this last year, the police investigations, the campaigns on social media, the leaflets handed out by Liz at London train stations or sellotaped to lampposts, and she might have been here all along, in the summerhouse at Creek House. If she is, it's nothing to do with Dom or Noah or the fisherman or a random, evil stranger.

But everything to do with us.

Everything to do with me.

Time speeds up and slows down again.

I kneel and push at the statue. It's too heavy for me to move by myself. I should call Charlie back to help.

I think about him waiting for me back at the house. Jem and Matt will be there too, ready for goodbyes. I bite down on my lip until it hurts. Last night was about closure for us all. About finishing the game and packing it away. For good.

We've found a way of being, of living, with *not* knowing. Of not opening up the box. Of not finding out.

The truth could be unbearable.

Unbearable.

I prefer Schrödinger's Kat. The one who exists in two dimensions. I shall focus on the one who got out of the box before the heavy statue landed on it. The one who took the money and bag and got a lift in a fishing boat to France, with the sea breeze in her long hair, exactly as she planned.

I take a last look at the angel's face and whisper a goodbye.

I pull the door shut and run back through the garden and across the lawn to Charlie.

"Ready to go?" he asks.

I nod. "Let's go, ready or not."

September 2019

A glimpse of red hair bobs ahead of me across the station concourse. I push through the crowd. I lose sight of her and stand on tiptoe. Hundreds of commuters coming and going. A flash of the hair disappears down the steps to the tube and I race to catch up. "Kat, wait! Kat!"

The red-haired girl is at the barriers when I get down the stairs. She drops her card and bends to pick it up, pushing her long hair from her face. As she tucks it behind her ear, it's clear she's not Kat.

Nowhere near as beautiful.

I stand still and breathe again, barged and tutted at by the mass of people.

I'll always see glimpses of Kat, or not-Kat. She'll be the person I see in the crowd when I'm least expecting it. The one who makes me do a double take, who makes me call out her name to strangers, grab girls by the arm.

I tighten my rucksack on my back, full of all I'll need. I'm prepared for rain and sunshine – down to a white bikini that takes up very little room. I pat my pocket to check my passport for the tenth time. My Eurostar ticket is safe inside my notebook.

I'll start at that bookshop Kat mentioned in Paris – Shakespeare and Company. I'm going to sit on the bench in the Instagram picture and wait. I'll get a coffee from the little café she recommended, set up the backgammon, read a book she liked, doodle a cat face on the last page. I may take a photo for our Instagram account. It's time for another post.

And I'll sit on the bench, half reading, half looking in the crowd for Kat to come.

I can wait. I have nothing better to do. I have all the time in the world.

Because people don't just disappear.

*

The late autumn sunshine casts long shadows in the garden at Creek House. Noah stands on the terrace and checks his watch. He needs an update from the builders before he phones the new owners. People like them have the money to rip out every last reminder of the previous occupants and to start again with fresh-painted walls, new furniture and a perfect landscaped garden.

It isn't so easy for people like Noah to rip out what's happened and make a fresh start. But maybe now is the time. That girl Millie hasn't been in touch again. Only Noah is stuck working out the past. No more. He really should dismantle everything in the boathouse. At the weekend he'll shove it into bin bags and get rid of it all. Fresh beginnings. New start.

The builders' digger has rucked up the lawn which Noah spent so long mowing into stripes this year. It's being turned into an infinity pool, making the most of the views. And the rundown summerhouse is being demolished today to make way for the luxury pool house. All this when there's a creek at the bottom of the garden and a sandy beach a short drive away. A colossal waste of money in his opinion, but at least some of it is coming his way. Things are looking up.

The loud noise of splitting wood and breaking glass echoing through the valley stops suddenly. The workmen stand in a huddle. One turns and waves at him to come over.

Noah swears under his breath. He planned to take his boat out while the creek was so still. Being on the water always clears his head.

He hopes this isn't going to take too long. He hopes it isn't going to ruin his plans.

It is such a beautiful evening.

Book Club Discussion Questions

1. How do you think Kat and Millie each viewed their friendship?

2. How are games used in the book?

3. Is everyone hiding their true selves?

4. Does Millie know deep down what happened to Kat before she arrives at Creek House in the summer of 2019?

5. Millie says no one would give Rob a Dad of the Year prize. But do any of the adults measure up as good parents?

6. How did the letters in Millie's notebook reveal her changing attitude to Kat?

7. Is Noah right that he'll be treated differently from the privileged Creeker teens? What does the future hold for him?

8. What did you think had happened to Kat at different stages of the book?

9. Would you have opened up the box?

10. What do you want to happen to Millie?

Acknowledgements

This was my lockdown novel. I drew on all the happy memories of Cornish holidays over the years and then twisted them into *Ready or Not*.

Thanks first to all at Little Tiger. To editor Jane Harris and Lauren Ace who have been unfailingly supportive in getting behind this book – even though I persist in writing stories with difficult timelines...

And to Dannie Price who puts up with all my daft marketing and PR questions with oodles of patience.

And to Sophie Bransby for another killer cover.

And to ever-helpful copyeditor Anna Bowles.

And not forgetting to thank Ruth Bennett who signed off the initial idea and chatted it through over coffee in my last pre-lockdown meeting.

To my agent Jo Williamson who never fails to be fabulous and provide the support I need.

To my writer buddies who became extra important through 2020/21 even if we had to meet on Zoom. Mega thanks to Tamsin, Jo, Emma, Anita and Christina in the Friday crew, and to my Saturday rogue critters Lydia, Amanda, Kate, Chris, Amarantha, Elaine and Steph. Their wise words and friendship helped me get this book down on paper and into a narrative. Thanks too to Chitra and my Write30 friends – can you spot the Friday writing prompt which became a letter in this book?

I'm grateful to the Arts Council for a Developing Your Creative Practice award, which couldn't have come at a better time.

To my beta readers Dolf, James, Ally, Tricia, Pete, Karen, Lydia and Amanda for reading the whole damn thing.

To Simon Harris who helped me on police procedures and interviews for the fair swap of Chocolate Oranges.

To Tania and James who helped me on Food lessons.

To my #bookpenpals at Channing School and Lurgan College. The enthusiasm of readers and school librarians is what keeps me writing.

To all my lovely friends. I can't believe how long some of us have been friends now – it's been decades, people! And I've appreciated you all more than ever these last couple of years.

To my family for all the encouragement, feedback and board games which fed into this book. I'm so looking forward to our next holiday in Cornwall. Don't worry, we won't be playing hide-and-seek.

1

A liar ought to have a good memory.

English proverb

They make me go to counselling. It's been a month already but I still have to waste my afternoon with Dr Harrison at Mandela Lodge. The guy's an idiot. Maybe these sessions would be worthwhile if Dr Harrison was any good at his job, or if I was actually upset about Hanna dying, but he's not, and I'm not. But we pass the time both pretending to be otherwise.

"If only Hanna had told me how bad she was feeling," I say. "I could've helped." I dab my eyes with a tissue from the box placed carefully on the edge of my armchair. It's for the weeping mob hanging round his office. Girls like Maya and Keira who are enjoying the drama of it all. "I knew she was upset about breaking up with Ed, but I never thought…" I trail off, leaving a dramatic pause.

Dr Harrison reaches out and pats my hand. "None of us did. None of us saw the signs."

He's the one with the framed certificates in psychology and counselling on the wall so maybe *he* should have spotted something. After all, Hanna used to see him because of all her 'body issues'. Hanna – the most beautiful girl you've ever seen. But I let it go.

"I suppose you never really know what's going on inside someone else's head," I add, blowing my nose and seeing that the irony's completely lost on Dr Harrison as he nods sadly and passes me another tissue.

"You're not to blame yourself, Jess," he says. "You were a good friend and roommate to her."

I don't blame myself.

I blame Hanna.

You see, Hanna set this off. She started going out with Ed. Not because she'd found her soulmate, not because she couldn't live without him, but because she knew how much I liked him – and that I'd never dare to act on it. It was just another game for her. And because she was always able to click her fingers and have any student here panting after her, she took him. Just like that.

I saw them together in the lunch queue, leaning in towards each other, whispering, a touch on the arm, and I knew. It was exactly 12.55 p.m. on June 14th last term. A pleasant twenty-two degrees and sunny outside. We'd done maths that morning, pages 72 to 78 of the textbook, mine had a coffee stain on page 76. Hanna wore pink Converse pumps, a cute flowery dress and... I could go on and list every last detail in the dining hall and describe every single person who was there that Tuesday but it would take too long. You'd get bored. Jesus, I'd get bored.

So back to the late departed Hanna Carlsen. I pretended it didn't matter – the rubbing my nose in it. I forced a winning smile. I whispered to her later that they were so perfect together, made for each other. And she flicked her white-blond hair and fiddled with her friendship bracelets. But I stored it up. It can be hard for me to move on – to not bear a grudge.

I force myself to refocus on Dr Harrison. He's now suggesting a tablet if I'm having trouble sleeping. I take a special interest in pharmacology and physics these days. I test myself for fun to pass the time while Dr Harrison polishes his glasses and drones on about post-traumatic stress disorder.

Question 1 (5 marks)
List the primary symptoms of a combination of alcohol, caffeine, appetite suppressants and low self-esteem.
Answer
Weight loss, blurred vision, tachycardia, nausea, confusion. (Open windows on the third floor to be avoided.)
Question 2 (5 marks)
How long would it take a teenage girl weighing seven

stone to hit the ground when falling from a third-floor window?

Answer

No time at all. Even a skinny girl like Hanna makes a hell of a mess on impact.

*

I never thought the whole Hanna situation would end like that. She didn't have to get so obsessed with how she looked, so thin-skinned about any criticism. But one thing leads to another. One lie rolls on to more. Unintended consequences. And life is full of those.

Now Dr Harrison's fiddling with his bushy eyebrows and doing that annoying tongue-clicking again. He uses it to fill the silences in our sessions. But this time he's the first to crack and speak again: "It's tragic when young life full of promise is ripped away." He speaks like a packet of fortune cookies. "Bereavement casts a shadow that's slow to fade." And another one. "But time can heal." Boom. A hat trick of clichés. He should go into the greeting-card business or cheesy calendars. Maybe he is already and that's where he gets all these platitudes. They're meaningless.

Doesn't he realize he's meant to listen as a counsellor, not dish out his opinions? But I can't be bothered to explain this to him. I don't want to shake his world order. He looks attached to his dingy study in this college in the middle of nowhere and his life with his mousy wife. She smiles out shyly from the photo on his desk. He's moved it from the middle shelf since our last encounter.

"You can contact me at any time, Jess. Not just within these sessions." He takes a card from the drawer and pulls an old-fashioned fountain pen from his shirt pocket. His nib scratches in the awkward silence. "But let's meet again at five on Thursday. I've written it down so you don't forget."

"Thank you," I say, lip quivering as I carefully cup the card between my hands. "And thank you for listening." I'm adorable. He loves this sort of rubbish. I swear his eyes are filling up as I close the door behind me.

I rip his stupid appointment card into tiny squares and let them flutter away on the breeze in the courtyard.

I don't need a piece of paper to remember anything.

THE
RULES

What if the person hunting you taught you everything you know?

"A heart-thuddingly nervy thriller." – *Financial Times*

"This tense, taut novel is chillingly believable." – *The Irish Times*

"Tense, suspenseful and explosive, Darnton's electrifying novel is a page-turner of the highest order." – Waterstones

Rule:
TRUST NO ONE

That's the strange thing about Dad's rules. I thought they were just his weird nonsense at first but then I realized I was following them. I mean, *choosing* to follow them – not just because he'd scratched them up on the massive board fixed to the wall. When Dad said *Trust no one*, he meant officials, the state, teachers, doctors, even other preppers.

And I followed the Rule.

I *still* follow the Rule.

I trust no one.

Especially him.

December 1

It's hard to imagine, but the Bowling Plaza is even worse than usual tonight. A giant, bobbing inflatable snowman is tethered to the roof, casting menacing shadows over the car park. Inside they've strung up cheap tinsel and 'Season's Greetings' banners, and a plastic tree with red and green baubles sits on the reception desk, getting in the way. It's only the first day of December, but already there's a sickly smell of stale mulled wine and a drunken office party is messing about by the pool tables.

Spotty Paul on shoe duty is dressed as an elf. You'd

think he'd have more respect for himself. I don't like doing anything where you have to wear communal shoes. I've had enough of hand-me-down crap. Paul sprays them with a sickly aerosol between each customer, but even so, it freaks me out. I shudder as I put them on. This interests Julie and she makes a note in her stripey book as usual.

"Maybe it's due to my feelings of abandonment," I tell her helpfully so she has something else to write down. "Or maybe it's because I dislike other people's smelly feet – which is completely rational, by the way."

Can you believe social services still has a budget for bowling and ice cream with Julie? The free ice cream would be OK if I was, like, six years old and on a beach. I'd rather have a double-shot Americano. I don't want a machine coffee in a plastic cup, so I stare for a while at the ice-cream choices to build the suspense before saying, "Nothing, thanks."

Julie looks disappointed. Maybe because she is now a grown woman licking a Solero next to a teenage girl sipping at a cup of water. I tell Julie she should cut back on the ice creams. If she takes all her clients out like this, no wonder.

"No wonder, Julie," I say, tutting.

Julie reddens and makes another note. Does she ever just call it as it is or does she always have some mumbo-jumbo excuse for my behaviour? "So who's drawn the short straw this year?" I ask.

"We're having a little trouble getting the right placement

for you after term finishes," says Julie, fidgeting. This is Julie-speak for 'nobody wants you'.

"How will Santa know where to find me?" I stare, wide-eyed. I see her processing whether I'm serious or not. She just doesn't get irony.

To be honest, I see the Christmas stuff happening around me like a trailer for a film I don't get to watch in full; like those adverts on TV where one big happy family sits down at a glittering table with a shiny turkey. It's not my world. I'm like the Ghost of Christmas No One Wants in a foster home. They have to pretend to like me and cover up the fact their own child gets piles of gifts from relatives who actually give a damn.

"So no room at the inn," I say, and laugh. "That reminds me of something."

"It'll be fine." Julie pats my hand. I shrug her off.

"Tell them it's only dogs who aren't just for Christmas – you can get rid of kids, no problem," I say. "Anyway, I don't know what all the fuss is about. It's just a day when the shops are shut and the telly's better."

Julie's Solero is dripping down her hand. I watch as the drip plops on to her lap.

"Can't I stay at Beechwood by myself?" I already know the answer.

The office party's getting rowdier, singing along to piped Christmas singles from last century. Paul the elf has to intervene.

I start bowling with Julie. "The sooner we begin, the sooner it's over," I say.

We take the furthest alley as usual, like an old married couple picking their regular table at the pizzeria.

I watch as she bowls. The ball trickles down the polished lane, heading slowly for the gutter at the side. She looks surprised. I don't know why. She's always rubbish at this. I used to think she was letting me win and hate her for it, as if my winning a game of ten-pin bowling would make everything all right in Julie-world. She keeps asking me if I'm OK, if I'm having a good time. Please! In this place? She's poking in her bag and casting glances my way like she's got more to tell me. I know the signs.

I win the game, by the way. I always win at things that don't matter.

"I have some news," says Julie, when we stop for her to take a rest and guzzle a fizzy drink.

Finally. What now?

"We've had a letter for you. From your dad. How do you feel about that?" She is obsessed, literally obsessed, with how I feel about everything. "We've struggled to find him, as you know. There was some confusion over names and information." She rummages in her briefcase and hands me an envelope. It sits in my hand like an unexploded bomb.

"If you don't want to look at it today, we can save it for another time. This must all be a big surprise," says Julie. She pats my knee. "Turns out he was back in America."

She says it like that's an achievement – like he's a film star rather than a waster.

STRIKE! The teenagers on the alley next to us are doing a moonwalk as the scoring machine flashes and plays loud music.

What am I doing in this place?

I look carefully at the envelope addressed to Somerset Social Services. The idiots looking for him must have told him where I've ended up. I flip it over. The return address is a place in Florida.

Julie checks her watch. Her concern for me only lasts until eight o'clock. She has to get back to her real life. She fiddles with her wedding ring.

I breathe. I listen to the clatter of the bowling balls and the whoops of another strike.

"OK," I say. "I'll read it."

I remove the letter from the envelope with my fingertips as if it's hot. It's oh-so-carefully typed, but I'm not fooled by him.

F.A.O. Amber Fitzpatrick

Dear Amber,

I can't tell you how pleased I was to finally have news of you. I'm sorry for your loss. I can only imagine what you've been through. But you don't need to worry about anything now – I'm here for you.

Your mom made it pretty difficult after we split up, but I never stopped looking for the pair of you. You know I'd never give up. I went to your old addresses, but you'd moved on every time. You always were a hard girl to pin down, Amber. I can't wait to see what a beautiful young woman you've grown into.

I look forward to rekindling that special bond between us.

Your loving father

"Short but sweet," says Julie. "He's been looking for you all this time."

There's nothing sweet about my father, but then she's never met him. She knows nothing real about him. About him and me. I promised Mum in one of her lucid episodes that I'd never tell anyone what he used to do to her … to me. He damaged her forever as sure as if he'd poured the alcohol and the pills down her throat himself. Some secrets are safer kept – especially when your dad's not the forgiving type.

It dawns on me that Julie's probably thinking Dad's the Christmas miracle, appearing to solve all her problems with placing me. She's seeing a happy reunion in Julie la-la land.

But that's the last thing I want. And now he's found me, I know there's no way Julie can keep me safe. Not from him. I can't rely on anybody but me.

"So how do you feel about your dad getting back in touch?"

Feelings again. Always feelings.

She checks her notebook. "It's been a while since you've seen him. We had a lucky break in tracking him down at last."

Lucky? He's always landed on his feet. Like a cat with nine lives. After all Mum's efforts with fake names and addresses to make sure the do-gooders couldn't find him, even when she was in hospital and I was playing foster-care roulette.

"Would you like to write back?"

"No need," I say.

"You may feel that now," starts Julie, "but let's talk about it again when you've thought some more. Maybe chat it through with Dr Meadows. It's a lot to take in, sweetie."

And as usual she's got the wrong end of the stick. She hasn't actually read the letter properly. She doesn't know how my father operates – but I do. Ten days have passed since the posting date. He'll be on his way – if he's not already here. I look around me, suspicious now of the office partygoers. I need to make plans. I have to disappear.

About the Author

Tracy Darnton is an award-winning author of books for children and young people. Her debut novel, *The Truth About Lies*, was shortlisted for the Waterstones Children's Book Prize and was a World Book Night title. Her second novel, *The Rules*, grew out of her short story 'The Letter' which won the Stripes YA Book Prize, run in partnership with The Bookseller's YA Book Prize, and was published in the YA anthology *I'll Be Home for Christmas*.

Tracy studied law at Cambridge and has worked as a solicitor and law lecturer. She graduated with Distinction from the Bath Spa MA Writing for Young People. Tracy lives near Bath with her family. She loves to go on holiday in Cornwall with old friends but she is absolutely terrible at hide-and-seek.

@TracyDarnton